"Hello, Marco. I heard you were home."

He didn't want to take his eyes off her, as his gaze took in the woman he'd never forgotten.

"You look fantastic," he said, and she smiled.

"Sophie…" He hesitated. "About the way things ended between us—"

"It was a long time ago, Marco, and I've forgotten it. I still consider you a friend."

He frowned. That wasn't the response he'd expected or hoped for.

"Have a nice visit," she said as she walked back toward her house.

Her voice brought reality crashing down on his head. She had been his once, but he'd left her. And now he would have to do all he could to win her back....

Dear Reader,

The joys of summer are upon us—along with some July fireworks from Silhouette Desire!

The always wonderful Jennifer Greene presents our July MAN OF THE MONTH in *Prince Charming's Child*. A contemporary romance version of *Sleeping Beauty*, this title also launches the author's new miniseries, HAPPILY EVER AFTER, inspired by those magical fairy tales we loved in childhood. And ever-talented Anne Marie Winston is back with a highly emotional reunion romance in *Lovers' Reunion*. The popular miniseries TEXAS BRIDES by Peggy Moreland continues with the provocative story of *That McCloud Woman*. Sheiks abound in Judith McWilliams's *The Sheik's Secret*, while a plain Jane is wooed by a millionaire in Jan Hudson's *Plain Jane's Texan*. And Barbara McCauley's new dramatic miniseries, SECRETS!, debuts this month with *Blackhawk's Sweet Revenge*.

We've got more excitement for you next month—watch for the premiere of the compelling new Desire miniseries THE TEXAS CATTLEMAN'S CLUB. Some of the sexiest, most powerful men in the Lone Star State are members of this prestigious club, and they all find love when they least expect it! You'll learn more about THE TEXAS CATTLEMAN'S CLUB in our August Dear Reader letter, along with an update on Silhouette's new continuity, THE FORTUNES OF TEXAS, debuting next month.

And this month, join in the celebrations by treating yourself to all six passionate Silhouette Desire titles.

Enjoy!

Joan Marlow Golan
Senior Editor, Silhouette Desire

Please address questions and book requests to:
Silhouette Reader Service
U.S.: 3010 Walden Ave., P.O. Box 1325, Buffalo, NY 14269
Canadian: P.O. Box 609, Fort Erie, Ont. L2A 5X3

LOVERS' REUNION
ANNE MARIE WINSTON

SILHOUETTE *Desire*

Published by Silhouette Books

America's Publisher of Contemporary Romance

SILHOUETTE BOOKS

ISBN 0-373-76226-7

LOVERS' REUNION

Copyright © 1999 by Anne Marie Rodgers

Visit us at www.romance.net

Printed in U.S.A.

Books by Anne Marie Winston

Silhouette Desire

Best Kept Secrets #742
Island Baby #770
Chance at a Lifetime #809
Unlikely Eden #827
Carolina on My Mind #845
Substitute Wife #863
Find Her, Keep Her #887
Rancher's Wife #936
Rancher's Baby #1031
Seducing the Proper Miss Miller #1155
*The Baby Consultant #1191
*Dedicated to Deirdre #1197
*The Bride Means Business #1204
Lovers' Reunion #1226

*Butler County Brides

ANNE MARIE WINSTON

has believed in happy endings all her life. Having the opportunity to share them with her readers gives her great joy. Anne Marie enjoys figure skating and working in the gardens of her south-central Pennsylvania home.

For Mary Alice
My roomie

"Few delights can equal the mere presence
of one whom we trust utterly."
—George MacDonald

Prologue

Had he heard voices?

Slowly, Marco Esposito opened his eyes, dreading the sight of the dappled shades of the jungle surrounding him. God, if he got out of here alive, he'd never wear green again.

He held his breath, straining to hear above the warbling, whistling clamor of the creatures in the canopy above his head. Must've been wishful thinking. Or hallucinating.

His tongue felt thick and swollen. It took effort to unstick it from the roof of his mouth. He was dying for a drink, but he'd finished the last of the water late yesterday. Kind of ironic, since he was soaked from head to toe by the steamy humidity in the air.

Something was crawling over his hand. He fought back a shudder and hoped it wasn't one of the brilliantly colored little tree frogs whose poison would finish him off a lot faster than the blood he'd already lost, considerable as he thought it was.

He knew better than to move, and not just because of threatening creatures. The pain was bearable as long as he lay completely still. He wanted to check his watch, but even the movement of his arm sent hot daggers of fire lancing up his right leg, so he didn't. He squinted up through the leafy veil of the rain forest that soared in a tangled jumble of vines, thick tree trunks and leaves overhead.

Daylight. Unless he'd been dozing a lot longer than he thought, this was the second day, then. Relief swamped him. By day the jaguar he so feared would be lying low, waiting for night, when its sharp predator's vision was unparalleled in the close, black regions of the terrain through which it passed.

He'd kept the flashlight on last night, shining it at random spots around him until the battery weakened and finally died. If he wasn't found today, the jaguar would find him tonight.

By rolling his eyes to the left, he could just see the humped outline of what had been a small plane, wingless and shattered among the ferns. The pilot was still inside, dead since the moment of impact. The other body lay on the ground beside the plane. He'd covered it as best he could with a heavy tarp, broken open a couple of capsules of ammonia and prayed that any passing predators would be too afraid of the strange scents to come too close for a while.

Grief tightened his chest. Stu had been a good researcher, a trusted friend and damn good on expeditions like this. He'd died less than an hour after Marco had pulled him from the plane.

Marco hoped he'd get the chance to talk to Stu's family one day, give them the final few words his colleague had sent to those he was leaving. Dammit! Stu had a wife, two kids, one of whom was still in high school. Life really sucked sometimes.

Family. His own family was going to be devastated if he didn't make it out of this green hell. He hadn't been home more than a handful of times in fifteen years. But in his heart, they were always close. His mom, dad, grandparents, four sisters... At least he wouldn't be leaving a wife or kids to mourn him, to try to get along on their own.

And just like that, she was with him.

Sophie. He'd tried to forget her, to keep her out of his head for nearly six years now.

He hadn't succeeded.

He could see her clearly: soft bouncy curls, laughing dark eyes, those full, pouty lips he'd so loved to kiss. He'd had no business kissing her, but his willpower hadn't been up to the task of holding her at bay after the first time he'd tasted her. They'd had only one time together but still he could call up the images, the scents, tastes and touches as if it had been yesterday. And the raw, naked longing that had sprung from nowhere had spooked him.

His only defense had been to stay away. Away from Chicago, away from his own home, away from the girl next door who'd said she loved him.

But she'd been too young to love anybody. He'd told himself that more times than he could count.

Sweet Sophie. Would she miss him if he died? Did she even think of him anymore? She surely was married by now, with a family of her own.

And that might be his biggest regret. He'd never thought he was a family man. But the thought of dying, of leaving nothing of himself behind to carry on his name, his blood, his life....

He hadn't let himself think of a family in years. It was

funny, though, that he'd never been able to envision children of his own unless they were being held in Sophie's soft arms. She was the only woman who'd ever even tempted him to think "family."

"Ho-o-o!"

The voice was close. It had to be, to carry so clearly through the sodden, sound-swallowing vegetation.

"Hello! I'm here!" He made the mistake of turning his head, and the movement jarred his body just enough to arouse the beast gnawing on his leg. He gritted his teeth; a guttural sound rose from his throat, and every muscle in his big body went rigid.

"Marco! Keep talking! We're coming."

He recognized the voice an instant before a head topped with flaming copper hair appeared from around one of the immense tree trunks. *Rescue!* Relief, excitement, panic that had been held at bay, all surged forth.

As soon as Jared Adamson saw him, he broke into a jog. "Here," he called over his shoulder. "Esposito's over here. The plane's over here, too." Jared leaned over him, shining a horribly bright light in his eyes, and Marco knew he was checking his pupils. "Hey, buddy. You have no idea how glad I am to see you."

"Wanna bet?" He was shocked to hear how hoarse and weak he sounded, but he tried to smile.

Jared dropped to his knees beside him, his face grim as he ripped an enormous backpack off his shoulders and began pawing through it. "What the hell happened? This wasn't in the plan."

Marco wanted to say something flippant, but suddenly he was on the verge of tears and he swallowed several times before he could trust his voice. Over his friend's broad shoulder, he saw several other rescuers moving toward the plane, unrolling body bags and transport stretchers.

"Engine failure. The pilot couldn't do a thing." He was able to speak again. "The others are dead. My leg…is bad."

Jared nodded, his hazel eyes sober. "I can see that. How did Stu manage to get out of the plane?"

"I pulled him out. He died after that."

Jared gave a low whistle. "You pulled him out? With this leg?" He shook his head. "Only you could manage a feat like that," he muttered as he bent to examine the injury. "You bandage this yourself?" he asked as he put one hand behind Marco's head and held a metal cup of water to his lips.

Pain threatened again, and he gritted his teeth. When it passed, he drained the cup before he answered. "Had to. Losing a lot of blood."

Jared grimaced, and his face contorted for an instant as he fiddled with gauze and antiseptic. "You did a good job." He took a deep breath, blew it out. "I'm going to have to stabilize your leg before I move you. Brace yourself, bud. This is going to hurt like a son of a bitch."

His friend's eyes met Marco's, and Jared went silent for a moment, looking away, struggling for composure. Finally he said, "It looks ugly. I wouldn't be surprised if the doctors want to amputate."

Marco froze. Deep inside, he'd known it was bad. He just hadn't let himself think about the mangled flesh and bits of bone he'd dragged together and bandaged the day before. "Save it," he whispered. His whole life was centered around the reputation he'd built exploring, researching and documenting geological environs. He'd suffocate in a sedentary job, a single location. "Please tell them to save it if there's any chance…."

"Will do." His friend's big hand came down over his

and squeezed once. "I'm going to have to touch your leg now."

"S'okay—" His voice rose to a scream as pain's teeth bit deep, and then the world spun in a red cyclone of agony that sucked consciousness from him.

One

Marco pulled the dark blue rental car to the curb a few yards from his parents' house in Elmwood Park, Illinois. He'd grown up in the Chicago suburb in this same house, and the familiar sight of his mother's red geraniums cascading from the window box above the single-car garage brought back a cascade of warm memories. The memories lightened the dark despair with which he had grappled since a doctor had told him his right leg would never regain more than a bare minimum of flexibility.

He reached for the manual shift, and then remembered he couldn't drive a clutch yet. Shoving the automatic gear into park with more force than necessary, he opened the door and swung his legs out of the car, being careful not to bang his stiff knee. It was pretty good most of the time now, as long as he wasn't reckless.

He took a deep breath, filling his lungs with the mild air. Early May in Chicago wasn't usually this pleasant. Better enjoy it while it lasted. As a geologist who frequently traveled the globe on scientific expeditions, he'd spent far more time in tropical climates than any other, and he much preferred the warmth.

His mood darkened again as he took his cane and walked slowly around the car. He hated using the crutch and rarely needed it for short distances anymore, but the flight from Buenos Aires had been long and tiring, and when he was tired, the leg was apt to give way without any warning. Slinging his bag over one shoulder, he started up the walk toward his house.

"Marco!" A screech of delight warned him a moment before the door banged open. Dora Esposito rushed through the screen door and off the small stoop with a speed that gave no hint that she was the mother of five grown children.

Her arms were around him before he could respond, and he put his free arm around his mother, hugging fiercely as he looked down at her ebony curls that had yet to see a strand of gray. "Still coloring your hair, Ma?"

His mother drew back, squeezing his shoulders and laughing. "Still as disrespectful as ever, I see." She wiped her eyes as she smiled at him. "I'll have to work on that while you're home. How long can you stay?"

He hesitated. "I'm not really sure."

Dora's face fell. "Don't tell me you're rushing off tomorrow like you always do," she scolded. "Sometimes I think you only stop by because it's cheaper than a hotel room when you're passing through Chicago."

He laughed, keeping his arm around her shoulders affectionately as they turned toward the door. "I'm not stopping off this time, Ma. I'm staying."

Dora Esposito was rarely at a loss for words, but his news struck her dumb—for a moment. "You're teasing your old mama."

"Never." He removed his arm from around her as they reached the stoop and juggled his cane into position. He'd learned the hard way that he needed all his concentration for stuff like steps, however small. "I have a temporary position at Purdue for the summer and fall semesters. I'll be around so much you'll be sick of seeing me in a few months."

His mother pressed a hand to her breast. "I can't believe it!" Then she realized what he was doing. "Oh, here, bambino, let me help you." She put an arm under his elbow and he stopped, forcing a smile. "It's okay. Ma, I can do it. It just takes a little time. Besides—" he forced himself to grin "—there's well over two hundred pounds of me and less than a hundred of you, so I'm not sure what you'd do if I started to fall."

His mother smiled back, although her eyes were shadowed. "I'll just go ahead and get your room ready."

"Thanks." Reaching the top of the steps, he grabbed the door before she could, holding it open for her. "I'm going to start looking for apartments tomorrow, so I shouldn't be under your feet past the end of the month."

"Under my feet?" His mother flapped a hand at him as she started up the stairs. "Since Teresa moved out, it's been too quiet around here. It's wonderful to have you home."

As Dora bustled up the steps, he set down his bag in the front entry and moved through the tiny house he'd shared with his parents and four sisters. The living room, on the left, was dominated by the large television he'd bought his father a few years ago, the better to view the Chicago Bulls during basketball season. The furniture was homey and practical, and his mother's needlework peeped out of a basket beside the sofa. Pretty crocheted doilies still covered the pie-crust tables.

In the dining room a lacy cloth lay over the table. One

wall was covered with familiar framed photos: himself and
his sisters, Camilla, Elisabetta, Luisa and Teresa as babies,
at First Communion, graduating from high school; his
grandparents and his aunts and uncles; his parents on their
wedding day. A vase of tulips from his mother's flower
beds brightened the room, and a crucifix hung above a
small table that served as an altar.

It was strangely reassuring to see that nothing had
changed.

The kitchen, too, was much as he remembered, except
that his father had installed the dishwasher all the kids had
given them for Christmas...two years ago? Had it really
been two years since he'd been home?

Yes, he realized with chagrin. It really had been. Last
Christmas he'd been in a hospital in Paraguay, fighting an
infection that threatened to undermine any chance of saving
his damaged leg. There probably had been ten tons of bac-
teria, at least, running around in the damned rain forest—
it was a miracle he hadn't gotten anything worse.

He wandered to the window over the sink and pulled
aside the lacy curtain, idly scanning the block of quiet,
well-tended backyards. All the neighborhood kids had
grown up and moved away—the once-lively street was now
a sedate community of grandparents who talked incessantly
about selling their little brick or locally mined lannenstone
homes and moving to sunny Florida.

As far as he knew, not one house had changed hands in
well over twenty years.

A movement in the next yard caught his eye.

My, oh, my. His male instincts snapped to attention. A
slender girl with shoulderlength dark curls was standing on
the little patio, her back to him, face raised to the early
spring sun, while a black and white cocker spaniel ran mad
circles around the perimeters of the yard. The woman had

a gorgeous figure, petite and full, long-legged and curving in all the right places. She must be one of the Domenico boys' wives. Though why a gorgeous package like that would tie herself to Stef, Tommie, Vincente or Geordie was beyond him. Grinning at his own wit, he treated himself to another leisurely perusal of the woman as more memories from his childhood swam through his head.

The Domenicos had lived next door his whole life. Their parents had bought the houses in the same year, and the next, each family had their first baby. He and the Domenico boys had been an unbeatable informal basketball team when they'd played pickup games with other guys on the block. He and his sisters had played and fought with the seven young Domenicos like one big family.

But they hadn't been one big family. And there hadn't been anything the least bit sisterly about his feelings for the youngest member of the Domenico clan.

Sophie.

Exhaling heavily, he leaned against the sink as pleasure faded. He still felt bad about the way he'd ended things with Sophie. He wasn't looking forward to seeing her at the surprise anniversary party his sisters were planning for his folks in two weeks. It was bound to be awkward.

Part of him hoped she'd married and had babies with some guy who loved her like she deserved. The other part...well, it didn't matter. If he'd dreamed of Sophie more times than he cared to admit over the past six years, it was nobody's fault but his own. He never should have allowed things to get so hot and heavy between them, and he never should have let her harbor any silly dreams about marriage. He'd known even then that the world's seductive call was stronger than any woman's allure. He was a traveler, loved nothing better than—

Sophie! He stood straight up and all but pressed his nose

to the glass above the sink. The woman on the patio had lowered her face and turned his way, and he'd seen what he'd missed before. It was Sophie!

Blood rushed to his head, and his pulse sped up. God, she looked wonderful. She'd been a plump little dove as a teen and young woman, pretty enough but hardly a stunner like this. He'd always wondered at the irresistible attraction she held for him, the strong reaction of his body to her nearness, to even the thought of her. She was nothing like most of the girls he had dated before her, the homecoming queens and cheerleaders who'd been happy to be on his arm.

Sophie, shy and quiet, was not like them.

But he'd discovered he rather liked his sweet little secret. Sophie, with her silky skin, little love handles and the abundance of soft curves she'd possessed, turned into a shameless wildcat in his arms. After he'd discovered her charms, the other women might as well not even have existed.

He stared through the window at her again. She had stuck her hands in the back pockets of the slim jeans she wore, and her body thrust forward in a way that outlined the plane of slender hips and flat belly and breasts that still looked lush and full. She was thin, much thinner than he remembered, but thank God she still had those beautiful—

Hey, buddy. What's it to you?

Sophie called to the cocker spaniel, who came bounding up the steps. As she turned and opened the door, the little dog disappeared into the house. A moment later Sophie followed.

His whole body sagged. He'd told her flat-out that marriage wasn't in his plans, had hurt her deeply and left her to deal with her hurt alone. He'd be the last person she'd welcome home with open arms.

A sound behind him alerted him to his mother's entry into the kitchen.

"Marco. Sit. I'll feed you." She paused, taking in his proximity to the window. "See something out there you like?" Her tone was sly, and her eyebrows arched.

"Very funny, Ma." He limped to the little table and parked himself in one of her cushioned chairs. "I'm thirty-six years old, not eighteen. I doubt there are too many teenage girls around for me to drool over these days."

"So who said anything about teenagers?" His mother's tone was all innocence. "A man needs a woman, not a teenager. You should settle down, Marco. Especially now that you—"

"Ma." His tone was flat enough to stop her in mid-ramble. "We've had variations on this chat too many times already."

She smiled, coming over to pinch his cheek as she set the table. "All right, all right. I just want to see my boy happy, is all."

"Hah. You just want to have more grandchildren than any other woman on the block." He gave her a narrow-eyed stare. "No matchmaking. Promise?"

Dora heaved an exaggerated sigh and sketched the sign of the cross. "Promise."

But as he dipped into the minestrone soup that no one else could make as well as his mother, he couldn't keep his thoughts from straying next door. He hadn't seen a man, and besides, his mother surely would have told him if Sophie had married. He wondered if she worked, if she had a steady beau, if she'd still melt in his arms the way she always had. No doubt about it, Miss Sophie Domenico was just what he needed to keep his mind off the inescapable fact that his days of exploring and roughing it in some of the earth's most inaccessible spots were over.

* * *

Sophie Morrell started when the telephone rang. Darn it, she'd just gotten comfortable after returning from her folks' home. Rising from the couch in her little condo where she had settled in to read a romance novel by one of her favorite authors, Sophie switched on the receiver. "Hello?"

"Hey, kid sister, whatcha doin'?"

"Hi, Vee." Sophie's tone reflected her delight. At thirty, her sister, Violetta, was only two years older than Sophie, and she had been Sophie's best friend since their childhood growing up in Elmwood Park. "I'm doing nothing, if you want the truth. I spent the afternoon with Mama and Daddy, then I decided to come home and prop up my feet and read the evening away."

"Did you eat?"

"Of course I ate." She laughed. "You worry too much."

"As your big sister, it's the job I take most seriously," Violetta said. Then the flippancy left her voice. "I don't mean to bug you, Soph. It's just a habit, I guess."

"It's okay." Sophie knew exactly what her sister meant. During her husband's illness, she'd spent all her time attending to him, pushing aside her own grief. Many days, she'd simply forgotten to eat, or been too tired to worry about food. By the time he died, she'd lost twenty pounds. She'd lost more weight after Kirk's death and only slowly had gained back enough that she didn't look like a walking skeleton.

While the method of weight loss wasn't one she'd recommend to anyone, she rather liked the end result. In the two years since she'd been widowed, she'd acquired eating and exercising habits that had kept her trim. She was proud that she hadn't strayed more than three pounds from her desired weight in those years.

Actually, it wasn't much of an effort. The clinic where

she worked, in a poor Hispanic neighborhood down in the city, kept her so busy that she often didn't get home until six or seven. And half the time, the workday ended before she remembered that she hadn't eaten lunch.

She liked the busy-ness of the clinic, though. Her work teaching young mothers how to care for their babies and be successful in the job market gave her many moments of joy. There was little she loved more than handling wide-eyed babies with mops of black curls.

And if she occasionally shed tears of anger at the unfairness of the life that had left her a widow with no babies of her own, she never, ever let anyone see them.

Of course, her work had its sad moments, too. But she'd lived through sorrows of her own, and, though she still missed Kirk, she felt that her life was richer for the experiences she'd had. She knew grief and rage and despair intimately, so she could offer the comfort of a kindred soul to others when those emotions came knocking at their doors.

"I have big news," Violetta said, breaking into her silent thoughts.

"What?"

"You have to guess."

Sophie rolled her eyes, though Vee couldn't see her. "I wouldn't know where to start."

"I'll give you a hint. Whose anniversary party is coming up?"

"Mr. and Mrs. Esposito's. But what—"

"And what handsome family black sheep has come home to help them celebrate?"

Marco was home. The bottom dropped out of her stomach and before she thought, she automatically defended him. "He isn't exactly a black sheep. He just travels a lot." Sophie wished she could call the words back the minute they hit the air, but too late. The realization that he was already in Chicago was more unsettling than she wanted to admit, even to herself.

"Sophia Elenora, don't you dare defend that man." Violetta's tone was heated. "He led you on and then dumped you for his silly little research trips, remember? You haven't seen him in close to five years—"

"Almost six."

"Okay, six, but my point is—"

"I get your point, Vee." Sophie sighed and raked her long hair away from her face. "I did manage to marry someone else, remember? You don't have to worry—my feelings for Marco were just a juvenile crush. They disappeared ages ago." She made herself continue in a light tone. "But it will be nice to see him again. He's been away a long time. Do you realize that this party might actually get all the Esposito and Domenico kids back together?"

"It's going to be wonderful." Violetta's tone had softened and she accepted the change of topic. "I talked to Camilla yesterday. She asked if we could spare a few hours that Saturday afternoon to help decorate the church hall."

"Tell her I'll put it on my calendar." Camilla was Marco's older sister, the one who'd done most of the arrangements for the upcoming party.

Violetta changed the subject then, and they chatted for a few more minutes before saying goodbye.

But as Sophie hung up the phone, she knew her peaceful evening was at an end. Most of the time, she deliberately refused to think of Marco. It was the safest way. But knowing that he was home, here in the very same city, had every nerve cell in her body dancing a kick line, and the memories came flooding back fast and hard through the gates that Vee's words had opened.

Marco.

Her stomach fluttered. She could picture his face as if he were standing before her, dark eyes gleaming with good-natured amusement at the world, well-sculpted lips and classic Roman nose, his black curls cropped ruthlessly short and dimples winking in his lean cheeks. His sisters had teased him about being a "chick-magnet" years ago—did he still project that same irresistible aura? Did those eyes still promise a woman secret pleasures beyond all imagining? He'd curled her toes every time she so much as looked at him.

And look she had.

She'd longed for him ever since she'd started to notice boys. Marco was seven years older than she was, and at eighteen, he'd already had girls lined up around the block. If he thought of little Sophie Domenico at all, it was only as the neighbor guys' kid sister.

But that hadn't mattered to her adolescent heart. He'd bestowed a casual kiss on her cheek at the party they'd thrown him before he left for college, and at the ripe old age of eleven, she'd been his forever. No teen idol's face had ever adorned her bedroom walls; Marco was the only man she'd fantasized about. At her Sweet Sixteen party, she'd been on cloud nine all evening simply because Marco had been home. He'd already finished his undergraduate work and had his first assignment as a research assistant under his belt.

That time, he'd kissed her lips before he left. Just a friendly, brotherly peck, to be sure, but to her it had been as good as a proposal of marriage. Though she'd dated through high school, she'd never gotten serious with anyone. Compared to Marco, all the boys she'd gone out with seemed like...well, like boys. Marco was all man, and her breath grew short and her heart beat faster every time she thought about him.

It had been the silliest thing, she thought, looking back. He'd gotten home maybe four times a year and most of the time, he'd barely noticed her. If he had, it was to tug on her hair and tease her. She'd watched through her curtains jealously when he brought girls home to family picnics, and she'd cried after she saw him kissing stupid Ella Pescke at the Espositos' annual New Year's party, a rowdy neighborhood event complete with dancing and enough wine to float a boat.

Then she'd turned nineteen. Her birthday was July nineteenth, right in the middle of the summer. Her parents had taken the family out to eat to celebrate. Everyone came, even her second oldest sister Arabella, Vincente's twin, who was overdue with her first baby. Some of the Espositos had come along as well, and Sophie had nearly melted into a little puddle on the floor when Marco walked in with Stefano and Tomaso, her big brothers. He'd just gotten into town and was leaving again in the morning, he said.

He'd winked at her and wished her a happy birthday, and her evening had been complete. She could have sat and looked at him all night. But right in the middle of the meal, Arabella's water had broken. While Belle's husband Lionel ran for the car, the rest of the family had gotten their food in doggie bags to take to the hospital and once there, they'd simply taken over the waiting room.

Marco had come along. "So I can give Ma a personal report in the morning," he'd said, white teeth flashing in a grin.

Sophie could still remember the stunned look on the nurse's face when she'd opened the door to tell them Arabella had had a girl. "You can't all be family," she'd said, falling back a pace.

And then, her prayers had been answered....

It was nearly dawn, and everyone headed home for some

sleep. To Sophie's delight, Marco slung a friendly arm across her shoulders as they all trooped down the corridor. "You can ride with me," he said. "Keep me company so I don't fall asleep on the way home."

She was too breathless, too thrilled, to reply. Marco had parked in the lot at the opposite end of the hospital and they left the others at the doors. He talked, drew her out until she relaxed, and they spoke of little things during the drive home: her college plans, his recent work with environmental geophysics in western Australia, their various siblings, most of whom were in the early years of marriage and parenting. They'd stopped at an all-night grocery and gotten sodas and talked some more. The sky was growing light and everyone else had beaten them home, from the look of all the parked cars on the street when they pulled up in front of their side-by-side homes.

He got out of the car and came around to open her door.

"Thanks for riding with me," Marco said. "Happy birthday." Then he put a finger beneath her chin and tilted her face up to his, pressing his lips lightly to hers.

It had been intended only as a familiar, brotherly caress, she thought, with the wisdom of hindsight.

But at the first touch of his mouth on hers, she lifted her arms to his wide shoulders and gave herself to the kiss, making a small whimpering sound of delight deep in her throat. Marco froze for an instant, and a part of her registered his shock. Then his arms came around her and he pulled her hard against him, fusing their bodies together in a breath-stealing fit that made her moan again.

He caught the sound with his mouth, tracing her lips with his tongue, then opening them for the masterful invasion of his tongue. Kissing her deeply, repeatedly, he stroked his palms over the soft flesh of her back down to the upper swell of her buttocks and back up to her shoulders until

*she was hanging limp in his arms, surrender a foregone
conclusion.*

*When he finally lifted his head, there was a look of utter
bemusement on his face. "Whoa," he'd said, breathing
hard, and she thrilled to the feel of his hard body against
hers. "I wasn't expecting that."*

*She blushed to the roots of her hair as she realized how
forward she'd been, and struggled to free herself from his
arms. "I'm sorry," she said. "It wasn't—"*

*But he shut her up in mid-sentence simply by kissing her
again, and as before, every cell in her body had recognized
him, and she responded with everything in her. When he
lifted his head the second time, he said, "I didn't say I
didn't like it, I just wasn't expecting it."*

*He paused, and an odd look crossed his face. She got
the impression he was weighing something in his mind, and
then he said, "Tomorrow night. Dinner? And a movie?"*

Sophie put down her book and paced to the window of
her apartment, looking out into the night as if she might
see him there. Altogether he'd taken her out less than two
dozen times, flying in for a quick visit in between assignments.

In between times, she'd waited impatiently. He never
called, never wrote. She never knew when he was coming
until she heard one of her siblings mention that he'd arrived, or until she answered the door to find him standing
on the other side.

It had been an unsatisfactory arrangement at best, and
she'd longed for the day when he'd be ready to settle down.

But that day had never come. One evening during her
senior year of college, Marco had come home. He'd taken
her out and told her gently that he wouldn't be coming to
see her again, that he was too old for her, that she needed
to forget him and get on with her own life.

She'd cried.

He'd comforted her.

And when he left the next day, she knew what it meant to be a woman. He'd been a wonderful lover, and she'd hoped to change his mind with the passion they shared, but in the end he'd gone just as he'd said he would.

And she'd been left behind for good.

Two

She had a horribly busy week at the clinic for indigent mothers in the Latino section of the city where she worked. And as if it needed a proper ending, in the middle of the night on Friday, Sophie received a call from a crisis management center that served the clinic's area. One of her clients had been beaten up by her boyfriend and was in the hospital. The young woman had no family, so foster care arrangements had to be made for her two-month-old infant.

She was at the hospital until dawn completing paperwork. The infant had been checked out by a doctor and declared unharmed, but all of the usual temporary foster homes were either full to overflowing, or she couldn't reach them.

Finally, around eight on Saturday morning, she got hold of a foster mother who worked with short-term emergency cases. The woman agreed to take the baby, but she wasn't available until Sunday morning. After a brief telephone consultation with her supervisor, Sophie received permission to keep the child overnight and take her to her foster home in the morning.

Fortunately she was prepared for such an event. This wasn't the first time she'd kept a foster child with her for a night or two.

She got home near 10:00 a.m. and when the baby slept, so did she. Unfortunately little Ana got hungry a lot sooner than Sophie did, and the nap didn't last nearly long enough. It was amazing how much time it took to accomplish even simple tasks with a baby around. She had to stop constantly to change a diaper, warm and feed a bottle, entertain when Ana fussed and rock her to sleep again in late afternoon.

Not that it was a hardship. She loved babies, always enjoyed helping with her numerous nieces and nephews. *Especially now that there would be no babies of her own.*

Then she remembered she'd promised her mother she'd come for dinner, so she called to warn her that a baby would be coming along. Edie Domenico, with thirteen grandchildren already, wasn't fazed by the prospect. So Sophie grabbed a quick shower while the baby girl still slept and stuffed a diaper bag with all the paraphernalia an infant required. Settling Ana in the car seat she always kept for such emergencies, she made the ten-minute drive to her mother's.

"Hi, everybody," she called out as she entered her parents' home, juggling the diaper bag, the baby and an extra bag of disposable diapers. She stopped to give her father's cocker spaniel a scratch behind his long, silky ears and when he promptly dropped and rolled over, she rubbed his belly with the sole of her sneaker.

"Hello, Sophia," her mother called. "I'm in the kitchen. Give that baby to your father and come help me roll out the pasta."

Sophie grinned. She suspected that her assistance wasn't as necessary as was her presence for a small gabfest. Her father was settled into his easy chair, and from the way he was fumbling around with the newspaper, she suspected he'd been napping behind it. "Hi, Papa," she said. "You don't have to take her."

But Renaldo Domenico shook his finger at her. "Are you trying to deny me a chance to snuggle that baby? And where's your kiss for your poor old overworked papa? Hmm?"

She laughed as she crossed the room and bussed her father's cheek. "How can you be overworked? You're retired."

"That's right," he replied, "And your mother thinks up more chores for me to do than I had when I did work." He took Ana from Sophie's arm with the ease of one who'd handled many infants. "So who's this pretty one?"

She explained Ana's situation to him and left them getting acquainted in the living room. When she entered the kitchen, she discovered that her sister Arabella was there already. "Hi," she said as she hugged first her mother and then Belle. "Where are the girls?"

Arabella and her husband had three daughters now. "Elissa had a softball game," she explained. "Lionel and her sisters are cheering her on. I begged off on the grounds that I needed a few childless moments at least once a week."

Sophie chuckled. "Do I detect a hint of exhaustion? Frustration? Mild insanity?"

"D—all of the above." Belle's voice was dry. "With the girls squabbling nonstop these days, moments of peace are few and far between." Belle's oldest two daughters were only seventeen months apart, and at ten and nine, they no longer played like little angels.

"This will pass," predicted her mother. "And then they'll be each other's dearest friends, just like all my girls."

Belle stuck a finger down her throat in an exaggerated gagging gesture. "Yes, Mama."

"Sophie, did you hear Marco's home?" Her mother pounded on the pasta board and muttered at her pasta in Italian.

"Yes. Vee told me." She steeled herself for the inevitable discussion.

Belle and Edie both looked up from their work. "And...?" said her mother.

Sophie met their avidly curious eyes with a bland smile. "And what?"

"Oh, come on," Belle said. "Did your heart go pitty-pat? Just the least little bit?"

"Of course." If she denied it, they'd know she was lying through her teeth. "He was my First Great Love. But I didn't swoon, if that's what you're asking."

"Humph." Her sister muffled a skeptical sound behind her glass on the pretext of taking a drink.

"I saw him the other night," her mother said. "He's still gorgeous. But oh, so sad, what happened. He'll never be right again."

"What happened?" Sophie repeated cautiously. This was probably one of her mother's little jokes. A ploy to get her to talk about Marco.

Belle looked up. "You know...the accident, his leg."

"What accident?" The sincere sympathy in her sister's voice was alarming and her voice rose slightly.

Belle's eyes grew round with concern. "Mama, didn't you tell her?"

Her mother was looking equally distressed. "No. I thought you or Vee told her."

"No," said Belle. "I didn't tell her. I assumed you—"

"Tell me what?" Sophie's sharp tone of voice cut through their twitter, and silence descended on the kitchen.

"Well," said Edie, "you know how Marco's always traveling into jungles and rain forests and deserts and—"

"Mama." Sophie crossed her arms.

"He was in a plane crash," Belle said hastily. "Everyone else on board was killed. He was rescued but his leg was torn up badly and they thought it might have to be amputated. But it wasn't."

"Oh, my goodness." Sophie sat down abruptly at the table. "You're not kidding."

"No," said her mother. "I wish I was. Cesare and Dorotea were frantic. He was in a hospital somewhere in South America. He didn't even call them until a month after it happened, and he refused to let them fly down. Dora sat here in this kitchen and cried her eyes out."

"Why didn't I know this?" Sophie shook her head blindly. "Where was I?"

There was a silence in the kitchen. "You were on vacation," said Belle. "It was at the beginning of October. I guess it just got overlooked after you got back."

"Yes, and you know how busy you are, *cara mia*," her mother put in. "I'm sorry. We just got our wires crossed, I suppose."

Sophie rose from the table. "It's all right," she said quietly. But it wasn't. She walked to the back door and stepped out onto the small porch, needing the fresh spring air and a moment alone.

At the beginning of October. The month was a difficult one for her. Kirk had died in October, and for the past two years she'd gone to a friend's cabin beside a lake in Wisconsin to grieve alone. It would suit her just fine if the month of October were erased from the calendar.

Then the shock of what she'd just been told set in. Images of Marco rose. Playing basketball, dancing a wild swing with one of his sisters on New Year's Eve, climbing the oak tree to bring down her stranded kitten—Marco was such an active, vital man. His whole life had been built around his physical capabilities.

He would be like a wild animal in a cage.

Her breath caught and she forced down the sob that threatened. It was ridiculous to cry for Marco now. His accident had been seven months ago. He'd survived, and if he'd come home for the anniversary party under his own steam, he must be doing fine.

A door slammed and the sound jarred her into looking around. A man stood on the back porch of the Espositos' house. A tall, broad-shouldered man with black hair—

And a cane.

He'd been waiting for the excuse to talk to her for days. Now that she was actually standing mere yards from him, the breezy greeting Marco had practiced flew right out of his head. God, she was beautiful. He stood there, staring like an idiot as she turned her head and met his eyes.

The impact slammed into his gut so hard he had to take a deep breath. Clearing his throat, he raised his voice to carry over the fence between them. "Hello, Sophie."

She simply stared at him for a long moment. Then she smiled gently. "Hello, Marco. I heard you were home."

He didn't want to take his eyes off her, even for a minute, but he wanted less to humiliate himself with a tumble down his parents' porch steps, so he tore his gaze away and concentrated on getting down the steps and over to the white picket fence as fast as possible. The whole time, he was conscious of her watching his labored progress, and the slow burn of helpless rage at his uncooperative limb gnawed at the lining of his masculine pride. If only—

No, he wasn't going to go there. He had a bum leg, a knee that had forgotten it was supposed to bend, flex and bear weight. That was reality.

It would get better than it was right now, he'd been assured, but he could never join his former colleagues in the field again because he couldn't hike over rough terrain and he couldn't carry a heavy pack of equipment for more than a hundred yards. He knew, because he'd tried.

That was reality. And thinking about the way his life should be would destroy him as surely as that damned plane crash had destroyed his leg.

He stopped when he reached the fence and leaned one arm casually atop one of the posts, forcing his inner turmoil back into submission as his gaze took in the woman he'd never forgotten. He hadn't asked about her once in the years since he'd held her last, because he didn't want anyone to think she was anything more to him than a good family friend.

It was for her own good. If she'd thought there was hope, he knew she'd have waited for him forever.

Still, he'd listened avidly whenever his sisters got to talking about the neighbors on his infrequent visits home. For a while, Liz and Luisa had gleefully brought up her name, rubbing his nose in the dates she'd had, but after the first year had passed, they'd stopped mentioning Sophie at all. He'd nearly broken down and asked them about her several times, and only the knowledge that he'd be leaving again in another day had kept him from inquiring.

Now, he wouldn't be leaving anymore. There was no reason to deny himself the pleasure that once had been his for the taking.

"It's good to see you," he said, his eyes wandering over

her slender body with intense interest. "You look… fantastic."

"Thank you." She slowly stepped down from the stoop and came across the small lawn to her side of the fence. "It's nice to see you again. Are you home for the you-know-what?" Her voice was hushed, in case his mother was close enough to overhear any discussion of the anniversary party.

"Yes, that and some other things." What was different about her? She seemed reserved and wary, not simply shy as she'd been before, and though her words were pleasant, they were impersonally uttered as if she were speaking to an acquaintance. It was probably simply that she was remembering how they'd parted.

He couldn't blame her for being mad. But still, here she was, and he was pretty sure he could charm her into forgiving him. After all, she'd said she loved him.

"I just heard about your accident." Her voice was still subdued. "It must be frustrating for you."

"It has its moments." He gave her his best unconcerned shrug. "How have you been?"

She appeared to consider the question. "I'm doing well."

"Sophie…" He hesitated. "About the way things ended between us—"

She passed a hand in front of her in a gesture intended to erase his words. "That was a long time ago, Marco, and I've forgotten it. I still consider you a friend."

He frowned. That wasn't the response he'd expected—or hoped for. This quiet, reserved woman was a marked contrast to the girl who once had hung on his every word. "I'd like to take you out for dinner, get to know you again. Are you free tonight?"

Her eyes widened, the brown completely eclipsed by a

blank look of shock, and he realized it was the first time he'd been able to discern any emotion other than generic friendliness in her eyes. "That's very nice of you, but—"

The back door opened behind her and they both stopped and looked at her mother, framed in the doorway. She was holding a very young infant cradled in one arm. "Sophie, this baby's starting to fuss. Shall I warm a bottle?"

She nodded her head, shoving away the hair that flew around her shoulders. "Thanks, Mama, that would be great. She ate almost four hours ago and she's probably starved."

Shock rolled through him like a fireball ripping through a munitions plant. Sophie had a baby? As he gaped, she swung back to face him.

"Thank you for the invitation." She shook her head. "But I have to get that wailing little one to bed. I was up half the night last night, and I'm hoping she'll sleep soundly." She smiled wryly. "So I can."

He nodded, unable to trust his voice. He was paralyzed by a fierce wave of rage that made his reaction to his injury seem mild in comparison. Who had dared to touch her? She was his!

"Have a nice visit," she said. "See you in a few weeks."

Her voice brought reality crashing down on his head. She had been his once, and she'd wanted to keep it that way. But he'd left her. Hell, he'd even told her to go find somebody else! He continued to stand, gripping the fence so hard his fingers hurt, and he could see her dismiss him from her mind as she hurried back across the yard and disappeared into her parents' house.

Slowly he made his way back to his own house, cursing the uneven ground. His mother came to the door as he mounted the steps, and she held the door wide. "Come inside and I'll fix you some lemonade. Is your leg bothering you?''

He wanted to snarl. *Not at all. Just because I hobble around like an old man, why should you think that bothers me?* But instead, he made his voice light and amused. "Knock it off, Ma. I promise I'll tell you if it needs a kiss."

She swatted his shoulder as he sat down at the table. "I see you talked to Sophie. She's still a sweet girl, isn't she?"

"Who's a sweet girl?" His sister Elisabetta came into the kitchen with a half-eaten banana in one hand and her toddler son sleeping on her shoulder. "Hi, Ma. Thanks for watching him today."

"Sophie is. And you're welcome." Dora plunked a glass of lemonade in front of Marco and picked up some more lemons for a second glass.

"Ah-h-h." Liz drew the sound out knowingly. "Still drooling over our Sophie, big brother?"

"A man can look," he said, forcing the turmoil that scrambled through him into hiding. But he couldn't resist probing. "Although I guess looking's all that's allowed now. I don't hit on married women."

Liz threw him a surprised glance. "Sophie isn't married anymore. Didn't you know?"

"I didn't know she'd gotten married at all. Who'd she marry?" He worked to project a mild neighborly interest. He was still reeling from the sight of that baby, and the implications at which its existence hinted. The thought of another man touching Sophie, kissing her, receiving the full pleasure of the hot, sweet response that always had been his threw a dark shadow over his thoughts, though he knew he had no right, no reason, to object. He'd been the one to walk away.

So why didn't that matter?

"His name was Kirk Morrell. They met in college," his sister said.

"It must not have lasted long," he commented. "Is Sophie the only one of the kids to have been divorced?"

"She's not divorced," Liz corrected. She threw a troubled glance at her mother, and Marco looked at his mother, too.

Dora's hands stilled over the lemons. "Kirk was a lovely boy," she said slowly. "He died."

He was shocked, and he let it show. "How?"

"Cancer." His mother made the word a curse.

Good Lord. Her baby couldn't be more than a few months old, so she must have been widowed fairly recently—

"Marco?" Liz still looked troubled. "Please…don't do anything else to hurt Sophie. She's had some rough years."

"I'm not planning on hurting her," he said, striving for a reasonable tone, though his sister's admonition stung.

"I'm sure you never planned to before, either, but you did," Liz said. "And all I'm saying's that Sophie's had enough hurt in her life. She's fragile."

"Thanks for the warning," he said, smiling. "I'll 'Handle with Care.'"

"I think we'd rather you didn't handle at all," Liz said under her breath.

Little sisters could be so annoying.

Later he was watching from his bedroom window when Sophie came out of her parents' house. He wasn't watching for her, of course—he wasn't that desperate. It was coincidental that the easy chair near his bed was beside the front-facing window. He'd been sitting there for over an hour, working on the syllabus for the course on glaciology he'd be teaching in September, when movement on the street had caught his eye.

She had a diaper bag over her shoulder, the baby in one arm and with the other hand she carried a big bag that he suspected was full of Mrs. Domenico's fabulous cooking. She set down the bags beside a little white compact car, then opened the back door and bent to strap the baby into a car seat. Her action gave him a clear view of the way she filled out her dark blue jeans as they stretched over her slender buttocks, and he swallowed, feeling his heart speed up.

So she wasn't married after all.

The thought of some other man touching her, teaching her about the pleasures a man and a woman could share, bothered the hell out of him, even though he knew how irrational that was. He was the one who'd left.

He'd wanted her worse than any other woman he'd met before or since. But she was the daughter of his parents' best friends and he'd felt guilty as hell when he'd finally let her push him into making love to her. And he'd known he couldn't offer her anything lasting. Leaving had been the right thing to do.

The thought gave him little satisfaction. What it did give him was a damned uncomfortable hard-on that forced him to shift uncomfortably in the chair. He could recall with vivid clarity the way her soft body had writhed beneath his hands, the way she'd clutched at him and held his head to her breast, the way her eyes had widened in surprise as sensations ripped through her and she dissolved in his arms.

Each time they'd been together, he'd struggled to remember that it couldn't be permanent. He'd known he was leaving, and he'd known he shouldn't encourage her any more than he already had. And really, it wasn't as if they'd had a long or exclusive relationship. No words of commitment ever had been exchanged.

But as she straightened and closed the back door, then

walked around the little car and climbed into her own seat, the only thought that kept running through his head was that he and Sophie had unfinished business between them. When he'd first come home, he'd harbored the stupid belief that Sophie would be waiting for him, just as she'd waited before, that nothing had changed between them.

Well, maybe she hadn't put her life on hold, and certainly he shouldn't have expected that she would. But she was single now, and so was he.

And he knew, without putting a finger on her, that together they still could generate enough heat to put the Great Chicago Fire to shame.

The following day was Sunday. His parents went to early mass at St. Vincent's, and for the first time since the accident, Marco decided to go to church. He hadn't been a regular worshiper in years, and if he ever went to confession again, he'd have enough penance to keep him talking for a month.

It felt strange to enter the church where he'd grown up, served as an altar boy and made his First Communion, strange to take a seat in the pew where his family had sat since before he was born. Now his four sisters were married or engaged, and sprinkled among the adults was a raft of his nieces and nephews. His older sister, Camilla, came with her family and as he watched, several of the Domenico clan slipped into the pew ahead of him where they'd always sat.

His interest picked up, but Sophie wasn't with them. Instead, the Domenico pew steadily expanded to two full rows, filled with a new generation ranging from a preteen boy that had to be Stefano's son down to a fussing infant in pink carried in by a man he assumed was Violetta's husband.

Sophie's sister Arabella smiled and blew him a kiss as

she took the last empty seat on the far end. He noticed she turned and looked toward the rear of the church several times, and when she smiled and beckoned, he glanced back to see Sophie coming down the aisle. It was an opportunity too good to miss. Before Belle could shove everyone in her pew together to squeeze her sister in, he stood and caught Sophie's hand as she stopped at the pews.

"You can sit here," he murmured. "I won't bite."

He'd forgotten how small she was. She barely came up to his chin, even in the heels she'd worn to Mass. She tilted her head up to look him in the eye, and he felt her subtly trying to withdraw her hand, but he only tightened his clasp. Her eyes were wide—the deep, rich chocolaty velvet that he remembered so clearly—and she hesitated for a moment.

But just as he'd expected, Sophie was too well-bred to make a scene in church, and after that first long, searching glance, her face relaxed into a small, cool smile. "Thank you," she said, and this time he let her have her hand back after he drew her into the pew.

When she sat, he followed suit, brushing just close enough that his arm grazed hers. It didn't escape him that she was quick to draw back, though they were both wearing jackets and it was as innocuous as a touch two strangers might exchange.

She didn't look at him again, simply linked her fingers in her lap, and he heard the rustle of silk sliding over silk as she crossed her legs. His gaze dropped and he studied the shape of her slim thighs in the pretty royal-blue skirt that matched her jacket. She probably hadn't lost very much weight, but what she had lost had enhanced the natural beauty that she'd always possessed and trimmed her womanly curves to hourglass proportions.

Then the service began, and guilt tore his gaze away

from her. He might have gotten away from the church too
much to suit his folks, but he had the superstitious feeling
that a lightning bolt might just seek him out for thinking
lecherous thoughts in a house of worship.

Sophie managed to ignore him during the exchanging of
peace between members of the congregation by darting up
to the pews ahead of them to greet members of her family.
It was, to his mind, a telling sign that she wasn't as indifferent to him as she'd appeared on her mother's back porch
the other day.

As he spoke the familiar responses, something inside him
relaxed. His mother's soft voice on his right side and Sophie's on his left, the shuffle and hush that accompanied
the rituals of worship...it felt right in a strange way, a way
he'd never realized he missed, but needed now that he'd
found it again.

When he finally limped back to the pew, he couldn't
kneel. Instead, he had to sit like the little old ladies who
were too feeble to get on and off their knees any more,
shifted to the edge of the seat with his back bent forward
and his right leg stiffly stuck out before him. His prayers
consisted mainly of a single desperate plea: Lord, please
get this over with.

And his prayers were answered. The service was con-
cluded swiftly. Sophie was out of the pew like a shot when
the postlude began to play. She immediately immersed herself in the crowd made by her large family, moving as far
from him as she could get.

He wasn't a particularly patient man, but he knew she
couldn't avoid him forever, so he allowed her to move
ahead of him down the aisle and out of the church. He
suffered through the welcomes of other members of the
congregation, watching her to be sure she didn't sneak

away, and when he saw her break off and head across the parking lot toward her little car, he went after her.

He was slow. He had refused to bring the cane along this morning because he was well rested, he reasoned, and getting stronger every day, and the doctor had told him to start doing without it from time to time. It was frustrating as hell not to be able to stride across the macadam and catch her at her car door. Instead, he forced himself to move carefully, and by the time he reached her car, she was buckled in and had started the engine.

She saw him coming. But until he walked around to her driver's door and tapped on the glass, she simply sat there with the windows rolled up. He put a hand on the door latch and then she punched a button, rolling down her window and smiling at him, though it didn't reach her eyes and he suspected it was only for the benefit of others around them.

"Hello again," she said. "Thank you for the seat this morning."

"We have a lot of catching up to do," he said, ignoring her casual words. "How about dinner tomorrow night?"

But she shook her head. "No, thank you."

It was a bald, simple response, delivered in a calm, almost flat tone of voice, and he lifted an eyebrow. "Okay, we can make it Tuesday if tomorrow night doesn't suit."

Sophie made an impatient sound, lifting her hand to rest on the open windowsill. "Marco, tomorrow night would suit just fine—if I wanted to go out with you. I don't."

"Is it because of the baby?"

Her eyebrows rose, and he thought he detected a hint of shock. "Excuse me?"

"We could take it along if you like." He'd never minded kids, enjoyed them, in fact, and though he didn't want to think about his Sophie in the arms of another man, he was intensely curious about her child.

She was frowning slightly, not looking at him. Her thumbs were rubbing back and forth along the edges of her steering wheel, and when he glanced at the small motion, he realized she was gripping the wheel hard enough to make the tips of her fingers white. "I didn't realize you had a child," she said.

Now it was his turn to frown. "I don't."

She looked at him then, and her gaze was cool and clear again. "Whose baby, exactly, are we discussing, then?"

Marco drummed his fingers against the side of his thigh. "Yours. I don't mind—"

"I don't have any children," she said. Silence lay like a wet towel for a long pause, and he thought she seemed upset. "I don't know where you got that idea."

"Your mother," he said shortly, not particularly liking the feeling of relief that coursed through him. He wanted her, badly, but it wasn't as if he couldn't live without her. "She came out the door the other day and asked you about feeding the baby. If it wasn't yours, then whose was it?"

"Oh, that baby." Her eyes momentarily softened and he caught a glimpse of something sad in her eyes before she stifled it. "That was a foster child who was waiting for a temporary placement. I'd picked her up the night before and couldn't place her until later Saturday, so she was stuck with me for a night."

"Doesn't sound so bad to me." At her questioning frown, he added, "Being stuck with you for a night." He leaned down until their faces were only a foot apart, trying to ignore the relief that had flowed through him when he'd realized she wasn't a mother. "Have dinner with me, Sophie."

Her eyes were wide and her full, lush lips slightly parted.

She ran her tongue around the edges of them, and her breasts rose and fell with the rhythm of her quickened breathing. The air between them seemed to hum with a powerful current of attraction, and he let his gaze drop to her mouth, lifting a finger to lightly press against her bottom lip.

She quivered for a moment, and he felt a small gasp escape her. Then, just as he was about to lean forward and seal his position with a kiss, she took his hand by the wrist and drew it firmly away from her mouth, all but flinging it out the window. "Thank you for the invitation but I'm not interested."

Though a lick of something—anger, mixed with a scary dose of panic—shot through him, he forced himself to smile lazily. "You used to be interested," he said softly. He reached in again and picked up her hand and brushed his thumb back and forth across her palm, trying to read her eyes.

But now she wasn't giving anything away. Her eyes remained cool, hiding any hint of what she was thinking. "That was a long time ago," she said. "I've grown up since then."

"Ah, c'mon, Sophie. Just dinner." He ran his eyes down the length of her body, chuckling when she pulled her hand away. "A little conversation, a little reminiscing…"

"No." She dropped her guard and shot him a look of such bitterness that he mentally staggered back from the heat, singed by the anger in her eyes. "I'm not interested in being your entertainment when you come to town anymore."

"It wasn't like that." He didn't care for the way she made his actions sound so…callous. He'd done it for her, dammit! "You were a lot more to me than just—"

"It's not important now," she told him, and the chilly

finality in her tone infuriated him even more. "I have a life of my own now, and it doesn't include you. That was your choice, remember?" And before he could come up with a response, she slipped the car into gear and started forward, forcing him to remove his hand or lose his balance and be dragged along with the vehicle as she drove away from the church without a backward glance.

His youngest sister Teresa was calling his name, and slowly, taking deep, calming breaths, he turned toward her, reaching for a smile though what he really wanted to do was punch something. Hard.

Okay, fine. Sophie didn't want to go out with him. He could work around that, and he would. He'd figure out another way to get her to accept his presence in her life. She didn't remember much about him if she thought he was going to give up and go away so easily.

Three

The knock on the door of her apartment startled Sophie.

She was sitting on the floor of her extra bedroom with a year's worth of photographs spread around her. She always had taken lots of photographs, too many, really, because then she felt compelled to organize them in albums. So she'd spent the evening sorting them into piles of family, friends and work photos, and she was just about to begin the unenviable task of sliding them into sleeves in the appropriate albums when a hard rap at her door had her jerking her head up and pressing a hand to her heart.

Hastily, she rose to her feet and tiptoed through the piles of pictures. It was eight o'clock at night. Who could it be?

She'd had Sunday lunch with her family after church and spent a pleasant hour with the members of her big clan that were present, but around two she'd made her excuses and slipped out, feeling the need for some breathing room.

Maybe she'd forgotten something, she thought, as she

put her hand on the knob and pulled the door the small distance it would open with the chain on. Or more likely, Mama had dispatched someone to drop off more food. Like she hadn't already sent enough—

"Hello, Sophie."

Marco was standing on her doormat. He was smiling, a crooked grin that reminded her of a little boy who'd been caught red-handed in an act of orneriness. But this was no little boy. He wore a light blue jean shirt tucked into a darker pair of jeans. The shirt emphasized the width of his shoulders, and at its open neck, dark, silky hairs curled out of the vee where the buttons weren't fastened.

The bottom dropped out of her stomach and landed with a jarring thud deep in her abdomen. Speech deserted her, and she simply stood there staring, trying desperately to keep her eyes on his face and not examine the rest of him the way she had longed to since she'd heard he was home.

"Are you going to invite me in?" His voice was low and amused, and she felt herself flush. He probably knew exactly the effect he had on her. He certainly had at one time.

That thought stiffened her spine, and she cleared her throat. She unbolted the door and pulled it open, but she didn't move aside to invite him in. "Marco. What are you doing here?"

He smiled again, easily, dimples creasing his cheeks, and a tiny fanwork of lines crinkled the corners of his dark eyes. "Visiting you."

"I don't want a visitor," she said, too shaken to be diplomatic. "Go away."

But before she could close the door in his face, he'd wedged his broad shoulders against it and pushed inside.

Her pulse sped up and she told herself the only reason she was breathing faster was because she was annoyed. But that didn't explain the heat building in her belly and radiating down to warm the apex of her thighs.

If only he didn't look so good, she thought, he'd be easier to resist. The fabric of his shirt looked soft and often washed; it clung to his heavily muscled chest and arms as intimately as she once had. At his lean waist, the jeans were buttoned beneath a dark leather belt. They fit him through the hips, snug and molded to the contours of his body in a manner that reminded her he was all man, and she swallowed as she hastily averted her eyes.

Dismally she glanced down at the oversize T-shirt she wore with the thigh-hugging exercise shorts she'd jogged in two hours ago. It was simple feminine vanity that made her wish she'd showered and put on something decent.

"You haven't even given me a welcome-home kiss," he said, his voice reproving as he arched an eyebrow, "and you're telling me to go away? Sophia Elenora, your mother would be disappointed in you."

"She'll have to live with it," Sophie informed him, "I have no intention of kissing you for any reason."

Marco shook his head, and his curly dark hair danced at the back of his neck. He'd let it get longer than she'd ever seen it, and she nearly reached out to stroke her fingers through the curls before catching herself. "Could I at least sit down for five minutes before you throw me out?" He grimaced, and suddenly she noticed the cane he'd used the first time she'd seen him.

"You weren't using that this morning." She indicated the cane, but she backed up and pointed to the pretty floral couch. He wasn't staying, she promised herself, giving him a mental boot out the door. Her system couldn't take his presence.

"I don't need it all the time anymore," he said, stiffly lowering himself to the cushions, extending his right leg before him. "Every few days I go without it for a little longer. Eventually I shouldn't need it at all."

She closed the door and crossed the room to stand behind the love seat facing him. "I guess now that you're in, you'll want a drink. Iced tea, beer, wine?"

"A beer would be great." His eyes were triumphant now that he'd talked his way into her home, but he was smart enough not to push his luck.

Without another word, she went to the kitchen, taking a beer from the refrigerator and getting an iced mug out of the freezer. With four brothers, she almost always had some beer in the house, though she didn't drink the stuff herself. Taking down a can of mixed nuts, she poured some into a little china dish, slipped the beer into the mug with just a hint of head frothing at the top, then carried the nuts and the mug back into the living room, plunking them down before Marco and reaching for a coaster on which to set the cold mug.

"So," she said, resuming her standing position behind the love seat. "Why are you here?"

Marco took a long drink, then reached into the dish of nuts, snagging one and tossing it into the air, then catching it neatly in his mouth before he looked at her again. "Isn't it obvious? I want to see you, Sophie."

"What about what I want? I told you I didn't want to go out with you. Last time I looked, the letters *n* and *o* spelled no."

"We don't have to date," he said.

"What?" It was the strangest thing he'd said yet. "What else would you call it?"

He hesitated. "Sophie...I need a friend. You and I, we could always talk. I don't have anyone else to talk to."

"Oh, come on." She made an impatient gesture. "You

have four sisters. Your parents. My brothers. And you're telling me you have no one to talk to?"

He hesitated again, and his hand swept down, indicating his leg. "Not about this."

She glanced down at the leg awkwardly positioned before him, and a wave of sad emotion crashed over her head. She knew she was going to drown if she wasn't careful. And yet...he looked defeated, hopeless, and she ached for the vital man she'd known before. How hard this must be for him!

"Well," he said, reaching for his cane. "I'd hoped maybe we could salvage a friendship out of the past, but I guess you're right. It was too much to hope for." He pulled himself slowly to his feet. "I'm sorry if I made you uncomfortable."

"Marco—wait." She rushed around the love seat and took his arm, putting herself between him and the door. "I'm sorry, too, for being so prickly. Stay. Please." She tugged at his arm but it was like trying to budge a giant redwood.

His face was remote and he didn't look at her. "No, you were right. I shouldn't have bothered you."

"You're not bothering me!" Hah. Beneath her palms, she could feel powerful muscles flex. Touching him had been a mistake. She was far too aware of the warm, rough scent of man, of the strength in the arm she still held, of the heat his big body gave off. Hastily she pulled her hands away. "Sit. Finish your drink."

He looked down at her then, and his eyes were full of warmth. "Thank you." His voice sounded hoarse, but she barely noticed as she watched him maneuver into a careful position on the couch again.

As he picked up his mug, she perched a discreet distance away from him. "So. How long is it this time before you fly off to the next assignment?'' She was proud that her voice was steady and impersonal.

His eyes shot to hers, and he assessed her over the rim of his beer mug. ''I'm not.''

''Semantics.'' She waved a hand dismissively, trying to smile as if he'd made a joke. ''Drive, then.''

''I'm not driving away, either. I've come back to stay. I have a temporary teaching position at Purdue, which will give me time to figure out where I want to settle. Since I'm not likely to get asked to join any expedition teams that go anywhere rougher than a parking lot, I won't be doing much traveling anymore.''

A fierce hurt slapped her at his last words. He was home to stay. But not because of her. The only reason he was settling down was because he couldn't manage the physical demands of his former occupation anymore.

Six years ago she'd have taken him no matter what the reason. But she'd grown up. She'd been loved once, and she had cherished it, though she hadn't returned it as she should have. She knew what it was to be loved, and she knew Marco didn't love her. He needed her, as much to help him forget his limitations as because he really cared for her.

No, he probably needed her for the former much more than the latter.

She wanted to send him away and indulge herself in a good, long cry, but she told herself she'd shed enough tears over him. He needed a friend, and as much as she'd like to kick him out of her life, a craven little part of her couldn't bring herself to deny herself the contact. ''You're going to miss traveling.''

''Yeah.'' He paused. ''But life goes on. I'll survive.'' A crooked smile twisted his lips. ''A fact that wasn't a certainty for a while.''

She couldn't help it; the thought of him lying helpless and hurting in a jungle somewhere, and even in a strange hospital in a strange place, brought tears to her eyes.

"Oh, God, I'm sorry," he said. "What a stupid thing to say—I forgot about your husband—" He lifted a hand as if he were going to touch her cheek, then let it fall away.

"It's all right." She wiped away a lone tear that trickled down her cheek. He thought he'd reminded her of Kirk, and that was fine with her. Better than letting him think she was shedding tears for him. "Do you want to tell me about it?"

He shrugged. "Our plane had engine failure. We went down not far from the Amazon. The pilot didn't make it and the other guy with me died shortly after we hit. I spent about a day alone before I was rescued."

She was horrified, and without thinking, she reached out and laid her palm atop his. "You lay there with two dead men and a broken leg for twenty-four hours?"

"It could have been worse." He was looking down at their hands; he turned one over and threaded his fingers through hers almost absently. The action sent racing streamers of heated awareness up her spine, but he seemed totally unaffected, and she forced herself to breathe normally. Just because the touch of his flesh against hers sent her body into a tailspin didn't mean she wanted to act on it. They were only going to be friends.

"How much worse could it be?" she asked. "Sounds pretty horrible to me."

He turned his head and slanted a smile at her. "Did I ever tell you what the rain forest is like at night? It gets dark. I don't mean the kind of dark in your bedroom, where your eyes adjust and you can make your way around. I mean pitch-dark, totally black. So dark that you literally cannot see a hand held in front of your face." He shook his head, still smiling. "A night can be a damn long time when your flashlight batteries are dying and you're wondering if a jaguar has been attracted by the scent of your blood."

She stifled a gasp.

"Fortunately," he went on, "the big cats must not have been hungry. But let me tell you, I was grateful that I didn't have to repeat the experience a second night." He absently rubbed his thumb back and forth across her palm and goose bumps exploded all over her.

"So then you went to a hospital." She prompted him without really thinking, too preoccupied by her body's re-actions to his touch to consider her words.

"And then I went to a local hospital." His voice went flat and dead, and his hand around hers suddenly stilled. "And if a good buddy hadn't been with me, I'd probably be walking with a prosthesis right now."

It was she who squeezed his hand this time. "I guess you were lucky to have him, then."

"I guess," he said reflectively. He gave her hand a final squeeze and set it back in her lap, then reached down to thump a fist against his thigh. "Although sometimes I wonder if I wouldn't have more mobility with a prosthetic limb than I do with one that's about as responsive as a two-by-four."

"It hasn't even been a year yet, has it?" she said. "Have the doctors told you what to expect?"

He nodded, and the black curls at the back of his neck whispered over his collar in a manner that made her want to smooth them down. "Supposedly I'll regain more flex-ibility than I have right now." He grinned, but she could see the effort it took. "But my dreams of playing for the Bulls have been dashed."

Accepting his obvious need to lighten the discussion, she

chuckled. "Your dreams of playing for the Bulls were dashed by Tiny Kniecki in high school. Wasn't he the one who beat you out of the all-state trophy?"

His eyebrows rose. "I can't believe you remember that. Yes, sorry as I am to admit it, ol' Tiny had some great moves."

"So did you," she said loyally, realizing as the words came out that they probably hadn't been the smartest thing she could have said.

There was a charged silence. Marco picked up his mug. "So you're a...what? A social worker...now?"

She nodded, grateful that he hadn't pursued her conversational faux pas. "That's what my degree is in. I work at a clinic for mothers and babies."

He grinned. "Which explains the baby you had the other day."

"Ana. Her name was Ana." Sophie shook her head. "She's in a foster home now, until her mother gets out of the hospital."

"Sounds grim."

"It has its grim moments. But it has many more rewarding ones. I really enjoy helping young women to get education and job skills, and to become better mothers."

Marco smiled. "I'll bet you're damned good at it. You always were a soft-hearted little kid."

They fell silent again, the implications of the last words echoing through the room. She hadn't always been a little kid to him.

"Um, Sophie?"

"Yes?" She looked at him again, and was surprised by the diffident expression on his strong features.

"Would you like to go to a movie or something? Just as friends?" he added.

She had to say no. She knew it, but she also knew that

when Marco turned those dark, intense eyes on her, she turned into the biggest sucker in a lollipop factory. He always had been like that, she lectured herself, with those warm eyes promising a woman the experience of a lifetime, those beautiful, full lips curling into a confident grin that told her he knew exactly what she liked most. Once, she'd taken that look seriously, but now she knew it meant nothing, and there could be nothing between them. It was best if she didn't see any more of him than family courtesy demanded. But...

"All right," she said. "A movie would be fun." About as much fun as leaping off a cliff in a dense fog, having no idea where or what you were going to hit when you landed.

"So shoot me," Sophie said to her sister two weeks later. They were knee-deep in buckets of fresh flowers, and she reached for a sprig of babies' breath, gently pushing it into the green oasis. She picked up the finished flower arrangement, eyed it critically, then sighed and set it in the shallow pan of water at the far end of the table. "He needs a friend."

"Friend, my fanny," said Violetta. "He wants you, Soph. A man who looks like that does not need women to be his friends. Anyhow," she continued, gesturing across the room with the pink carnation she held, "it looks to me like he has plenty of friends."

And Sophie had to admit that it did. Marco, her brothers Vince and Tom and one of his brothers-in-law were setting up tables for the evening's anniversary party for her parents. Coming along behind them, opening the folding chairs and placing them along the rows of tables, were her other two brothers.

Marco's sister Camilla stood in the middle of the floor,

directing her husband as he struggled to attach crepe paper streamers and wedding bells to the big overhead light in the parish hall. Arabella and Marco's two youngest sisters followed along behind the group of men, covering the tables with pink paper, taping it securely as they worked.

"I mean, with the size of these two families, why does he want to talk to you?" Violetta asked. Then her face reddened. "That wasn't an insult."

"Gee, thanks," said Sophie dryly. "I feel so much more…valued now."

"You know what I mean." Vee aimed another carnation at her. "He grew up with our brothers."

"He and I share some history, too," Sophie reminded Violetta. "And I guess he's used to talking to me about most anything. Stop worrying. We're just friends." And they were. Twice in the past two weeks they'd gone to the movies; once they'd driven over to al Gelato on Harlem for delicious homemade ice cream. In the past they would have walked, but Marco's leg wasn't up to a hike of many blocks yet.

They'd gotten along well together, she thought. She'd enjoyed telling him about recent events at work, and he'd entertained her with descriptions of the apartments he'd looked at. They'd argued about the Bulls' chances of beating the Bullets, and whether or not the Sox had a deep enough bull pen to draw on throughout the baseball season. She'd caught him up on the doings of mutual friends and old neighbors; he'd regaled her with previously untold stories of her brothers' wild escapades from high school. Of which he hadn't taken part, naturally.

And if her heart beat a little faster every time he casually took her hand, only she knew. After the movie they'd seen on Thursday evening, he'd driven her home. It was the one point on which Marco was completely, ridiculously inflexible.

"We can take turns driving," she'd suggested. "Fiftyfifty. That's what friends do."

"I don't care." His air of lazy amusement and good humor had fallen away abruptly, and she'd caught a glimpse of the iron will that hid beneath. "Men drive women. I drive you."

"You Tarzan, me Jane?" she'd teased, trying to regain their former compatible conversation.

"Call me whatever you like. I won't have you driving around the city alone at night."

"Oh, so you'd let me drive if we went somewhere, say, on a Saturday afternoon?" Hah. She had him there.

But he hadn't turned a hair. "Nope. My father raised a gentleman. No lady ever gets behind the wheel when she's with me."

Sophie had stared at him across the confines of the car as he'd parked in front of her building. "That's a pigheaded, chauvinistic attitude."

"Yeah." As fast as it had fled, his good humor had returned. "Oink, oink."

He'd stopped the car and walked her to the door as he had each of the other two times they'd gone out. On each of the other occasions, he'd done little more than touch her elbow when he said good-night, so she wasn't prepared when he looked down at her and said, "I like being with you, Sophie."

Then he'd cupped her elbows in his big palms and bent toward her. As his head had blocked out the streetlight behind him, her eyes had fluttered closed and she'd tensed, her whole body focused on the coming kiss.

But to her surprise, he'd only brushed her cheek with his lips, a quick, almost impersonal peck, before wheeling and heading back to the car. "See you Saturday," he'd called over his shoulder.

"See you Saturday," she'd echoed, exhaling a long breath of what she told herself was relief, before she'd let herself in to her cozy, comfortable condo.

But once inside, she couldn't seem to get Marco out of her mind. They were only friends now, she reminded herself as she brushed her teeth.

But you were more than friends once.

For the first time in a very long time, she allowed herself to think about the first and only night they'd been intimate. Marco had come home that morning. He was leaving the next day and when he'd asked her out to dinner, she'd dropped any plans she'd had to spend the evening with him....

After the meal he took her to see a new movie starring two of the young, hot properties of that time. Unfortunately, the suspense thriller also had several scenes where the hero and heroine burned off their sexual tension together.

Initially she was acutely embarrassed to be sitting with Marco, watching two people make love. Then, on the heels of embarrassment, came arousal. Her body felt overheated and her skin so sensitive she could hardly bear the places where her clothing clung. Her breasts felt heavy; she struggled to keep her breathing even; between her thighs throbbed an unfamiliar sensation that slowly drew her abdomen into a taut knot.

Halfway through the scene, Marco suddenly shot to his feet. "C'mon," he muttered. Grabbing her hand, he all but dragged her out of the theater.

Neither of them spoke a word as they went back out on the street, walking toward the car, which was parked two blocks away. He took her out of the city, toward Elmwood, but a few minutes before their exit, he turned off the free-way and drove a short distance to a small park.

When he stopped the car, he came around to her side and took her hand, leading her down a path to sit on a bench by the side of a little lake. His arm was around her; her head rested in the curve of his shoulder. It felt as if it had been made for her, and she gave a quiet sigh of contentment.

Then he shifted, turning her into his arms and seeking her mouth, and her contentment changed instantly to a breathless sensual state in which she was his to do with as he liked, his to caress and kiss and fondle.

His hands tightened at her waist and he lifted her into his lap, pressing her backward over one hard arm while his lips continued to ravage hers, his tongue seeking hers and drawing it back into the hot cavern of his own mouth. One big hand slipped beneath the short sweater she'd paired with her skirt and she jolted against him when she felt his warm palm on her bare skin, smoothing over her ribs, a finger slipping stealthily in a circle around her navel. She jolted again when the palm moved upward and he covered one breast and explored the soft mound with his hand, using his thumb to tease the aching tip until she was squirming and writhing in his arms.

"Sophie," he murmured against her lips. "Tell me to stop." But his thumb continued its steady caress even as he spoke.

"No." She still clutched his shoulders as his touch made her shudder with pleasure. He'd touched her like this before, petting and stroking her until they were both panting like they'd run a five-minute mile, but always, always he stopped. She didn't want him to stop this time.

He shuddered, his big body shaking with his efforts at

control. *"You're no help at all."* There was amusement in his voice, but it was rough with suppressed desire.

Then, so slowly that it was torture, he withdrew his hand from beneath her top. His lips made shallower forays over her mouth and finally, he lifted his head and set her gently on the bench beside him, though he kept her closely snuggled against his body.

When she risked a glance at his profile, she saw he was frowning. All she wanted was to be somewhere private and dark, somewhere where he could continue to enthrall her body with the magic of his caresses, but the look on his face concerned her.

"What's wrong?" she'd asked.

Marco had shaken his head. *"Us. Me. All these years, you've been sweet little Sophie, the girl next door. And now all I can think about is how soon I'm going to get my hands on you again."*

"That's simple," she said, greatly daring. *"Just reach out and touch."* She took his hand and placed it over her breast again, sucking in a breath of delight when his fingers automatically shaped the tender mound.

"Sophie!" His breathing was ragged. *"You're supposed to slap my face now, not aid and abet my lecherous thoughts."*

"But I like your lecherous thoughts," she said.

He laughed, but it was a sound of frustration as much as amusement. He stood and reached down, hauling her to her feet and into his arms. *"You're playing with fire, baby."* His hips thrust against her soft belly in graphic demonstration, and she felt the bulge of his erection pushing out his pants. *"I want more than a few kisses."*

"All right." And it was. She'd known since forever that she was Marco's. It was wonderful that he'd finally begun to want her, too.

"It's not all right." It was practically a snarl. He released her and raked a hand through his ebony curls in utter frustration. *"You're a virgin, aren't you?"* The words were almost an accusation.

She blushed. *"Yes, but—"*

"Stop right there." He spun away from her and his shoulders were tense and stiff as he stared out over the lake. *"I'm leaving tomorrow, Sophie. And I won't be back for God knows how long. I'm not in the habit of using young girls and then tossing them aside."*

"I'm not a girl." Her words were soft but insistent. *"I'm a woman, and I can make my own decision about what I want."*

"I can't stay," he said, desperation in his tone.

"I'm not asking you to," she said, though in her heart she longed for exactly that. She slipped around in front of him again. *"Each time you leave, I wonder if you'll ever come back. I want some memories to keep me warm when you're gone again."* She put her arms around his neck and pressed herself against him. When he continued to stand still as a statue, she took a deep breath, reaching down between them and placing her palm over the firm male flesh she'd aroused. *"Please, Marco, make love to me."*

And he had. Oh, God, he had. Right there, on a grassy bank by the lake. He'd been tender, easing her into womanhood so gently that she'd barely felt any pain. He'd taught her what her body was made for that night, over and over until dawn pearled the sky and they were both drooping with exhaustion.

And then he'd left her.

Her hand stilled, and the washcloth she'd been holding slipped from her grasp. She'd been so sure, ridiculously confident that she could hold him with her body.

But he'd left, just as he'd planned. And just as he'd promised, he hadn't come home again.

As the tears began to fall, she stumbled toward her bed, collapsing across it in a violent storm of grief.

Four

He hadn't worn a suit in almost two years. Normally, the black pinstriped one he'd chosen was New Year's Eve dress, but last year, he'd spent New Year's Eve in a rehab hospital, coming to grips with the fact that he'd never be climbing another mountain or hiking through another rain forest or crossing a veld.

It was a bit tight across the shoulders, and he knew why. Since his exercise options were limited now, he'd been swimming—and lifting weights—every day. Both were activities guaranteed to pack on the muscle through the chest and upper arm. He looked at himself in the mirror that had hung in the upstairs hall since his sisters first had become fashion-conscious teenagers. Not bad, though. He'd do.

But he'd give up the extra muscle for a good leg in a heartbeat.

He snorted. Looking in a mirror. He was pitiful. If his buddy Jared could see him now, he'd be rolling on the floor. Still, as he adjusted the red-patterned tie, he admitted to himself that he wanted to look good tonight. He wanted Sophie to open her door and stop dead when she saw him.

Even a second glance would be nice.

He sighed as he slowly took the steps down and grabbed his keys, then headed out the door to his car. At least he didn't have to sneak out. Camilla and Mike had asked his parents to go out to dinner at an elegant restaurant as their anniversary gift, and then his folks thought they were stopping by the church to celebrate another church member's birthday. Camilla had even gone so far as to have an invitation to the mythical event made—it had been on his mother's refrigerator since he'd been home.

He drummed his fingers on the wheel impatiently as he waited through several red lights driving the dozen or so blocks to Sophie's condo. He'd had a hard time convincing Sophie that he should drive her to the party. But there was no way he was letting her drive around alone at night. Hell, he even hated the thought of her driving downtown alone during the day.

Yeah, a second glance would be a breakthrough. Since the night he'd talked her into going out with him under the guise of needing a friend, she'd treated him gently, kindly, sweetly, but without a hint of the sexual awareness that was making him crazier every time he saw her. The only time he sensed her feelings about him weren't as casual as they appeared was when he touched her. He was determined to get her used to the feel of his hands on her again. And touching her, without really touching her the way he wanted, was pushing his willpower to its outer limits. The other night he'd barely restrained himself from grabbing her and kissing her senseless. A quick peck on the cheek and a hasty retreat were all that saved her.

Or him. She might never speak to him again if he rushed her like that.

And he didn't want to spook her. He'd assumed—stupidly—that once he got her alone he'd be able to talk her into resuming some sort of relationship with him. But at church, and when he'd shown up at her apartment, Sophie had been firmer and more prickly that he'd ever seen her, and he'd realized if he didn't change his tactics, she was going to boot him out on his ear.

Hence, this friendship stuff. He had to start somewhere.

He knew exactly where he'd like to start, had since she'd opened the door and he'd thought she was wearing nothing but that old T-shirt. Even after he'd seen the brief shorts peeking from beneath it, it was all he could do to put words together in coherent sentences. Occasionally he felt mildly guilty for using her sympathy and compassion to manipulate her, but he knew, he *knew* that once she'd accepted his presence in her life they could have their old relationship back.

He parked the car and walked to her door, carrying the long-stemmed white rose he'd bought on impulse earlier in the day when he'd gone with Teresa and Lu to pick up the flowers. His sisters had teased him unmercifully until he'd threatened to dunk both of their heads in the big sink where they unloaded the flowers at the church.

Almost before he pressed the bell, Sophie opened the door. "Hi. You can come in for a minute. I don't want to be late. I'm ready as soon as I go and get my—what?"

He'd taken her by the elbow and begun to turn her in a circle, mostly to hide the shock that he knew had to be on his face. "That's, um, some dress."

"Oh. Thanks, if that was supposed to be a compliment." She linked her fingers together.

"It was." He cleared his throat. Damn, why was it that

his brain seemed to short-circuit every time she was around? He used to have the smoothest lines in town.

Drawing the white rose from behind his back, he held it out to her. "Here."

Her eyes widened. She eyed the blossom for a long moment before accepting it, but her voice was steady when she spoke. "Thank you." As she looked back down at the rose, he took the chance to study her again.

She was wearing a simple black dress in some sort of satiny fabric, with long sleeves. It should have been no big deal. And maybe it wouldn't be, if the dress didn't have a neckline that barely clung to her smooth, bare shoulders and plunged down to showcase a truly incredible expanse of snowy cleavage. Or if it hadn't flowed over her curves like ebony paint. Or if the black heels she wore didn't make her legs look ten miles long beneath the short hemline.

"You look beautiful," he told her, clearing his throat again to dislodge the boulder that seemed to be stuck in there.

She stared up at him uncertainly. "Thank you. You look pretty sharp yourself." Then she walked across the room and picked up a small evening bag. "Shall we go?"

He thrust his hands into the pockets of his pants to keep from reaching for her, and instead reached for the teasing flirtation he used to be so good at delivering. "I suppose. Unless you'd rather stay here and let me peel you out of that dress and ravish you."

She laughed. "An irresistible offer. But your sisters will be unhappy if you don't show up for this party." Her tone was as light and teasing as his had been, and her momentary uncertainty seemed to have disappeared. "And trust me, you don't want four women all hunting your head at the same time."

He chuckled. "Nope. Been there, done that."

The amusement drained out of her face, and it was as if she'd turned off a light behind her eyes. "And I bet they weren't your sisters, either." Opening the door, she preceded him out to the car before he could come up with a response.

But as he rounded the hood and carefully folded himself, stiff leg first, into the car, a small flower of satisfaction began to bloom within him. For the first time he thought there was a chance she might still harbor some feelings for him. Unless he was mistaken, that note in her voice had been jealousy.

And he was rarely mistaken about women.

They got to the church with plenty of time to spare, and Sophie immediately joined his sisters in the last moments of frantic preparation. Where was the spoon for the crystal dish? Could somebody climb up there and fix that streamer that fell down? Were the flowers around the cake arranged to everyone's liking?

He stood back, well out of the way with her four brothers and watched the women fuss. Only he mostly was watching Sophie's figure as she bustled around the room. Once, when she leaned over the cake table and the hemline of the black dress rose perilously high, it was all he could do to keep from rushing over there and tugging it down again.

Or whisking her off to a private place and tugging it off, which sounded like a much better idea.

Other guests began to arrive, and Sophie slipped among them, greeting old friends and welcoming others. His jaw hurt from gritting his teeth when one guy's hand strayed far too close to her bottom when he hugged her. If he hadn't seen Sophie reach back and snag the jerk's wrist, he might have gone over there and decked him.

By the time they all stood back to wait for his parents, he was thoroughly out of humor. When she came within reach, he grabbed for her hand and pulled her close to his side, twining his fingers with hers. "Stay here."

"Why?" She turned to stare at him. Then her brow furrowed with concern. "You've been standing an awfully long time. Let me get you a chair."

"I don't want a chair." He forced a grin, though it galled him that she thought she had to baby him. He was the one who was supposed to be the caretaker, dammit. "I'm fine. I just want you next to me."

"Oh." She considered that, then shrugged. "I guess friends should stick together."

He had just about had it with this friends business. Couldn't she see that he was interested in more than that? He was pretty sure she wasn't indifferent to him. She might not be ready to admit it, but the fire still burned between them. So why was she denying them both the pleasure he knew they could share?

Was it all because he'd left when they were younger? Fine. He'd explain it to her again, explain how guilty he'd felt at the uncontrollable lust that had raged within him for his buddies' little sister. Explain that she would never have been happy traipsing around the globe after him, or worse, waiting in a shack in some grungy little town for him to come back from whatever expedition he was on.

His fingers tightened around hers and she looked up at him in inquiry—

And then Camilla threw open the doors and ushered his parents into the room.

"SURPRISE!"

From that moment onward, the party was craziness. Tears to blot, corsages to pin in place, cake to pass, champagne and toasts, endless family photos… By the time the small combo that Camilla had hired began to play some dance tunes, he had had enough party to last him for a long time. His leg ached from standing too long, but he'd be damned if he'd sit down like an invalid while people clucked and fussed over him.

Finally, as the dance floor filled with people and his parents began to circulate and talk with all their guests, he limped to the edge of the room, where two large pillars and a beautiful stand of ferns and small potted trees hid a secluded corner. It could be seen from the hallway that led to the rest rooms, but if he sat on the windowsill near the farthest pillar back, he doubted anyone would even notice him.

He noticed them, though. The combo played a surprisingly upbeat variety of songs, and his body wanted to move with the rhythms. He'd been a hell of a dancer—before. It was fun, and it was a great way to get dates, too. Women adored guys who could dance, so it was a skill he'd cultivated.

Besides, with four sisters, he'd learned whether he liked it or not.

But his dancing days were past. Anger, deep and hot, rose within him. This wasn't fair, dammit. He realized his hands were in fists and he made a conscious effort to uncurl them—

"Marco?"

It was Sophie, poised at the edge of the greenery like a doe testing the safety of a meadow. Ready for flight at any moment.

"Are you all right?" She came a little farther into his corner after glancing around, and he realized she was checking to be sure he was alone.

"I'm fine." But try as he might, he couldn't inject a carefree note into his voice, couldn't get past the frustrations roiling within him.

"You don't sound fine." Crossing the small space, she

rested a hip against the windowsill and turned toward him, her wide eyes searching his face. "Does your leg hurt?"

Her gentle concern took the rage out of him, replacing it with resignation. "A little bit," he said.

"I knew it. Even from across the room I could tell there was something wrong. Would you like to leave? I could drive—"

He grinned and picked up her hand. "Always trying to figure out a way to get behind the wheel, aren't you?" Carefully, he slid off the windowsill until he was leaning back against it. He indicated the crowded floor beyond the palms, still holding her small fingers in his. "The truth is, I'm having a Feel Sorry for Marco party in here. I used to enjoy dancing."

"I remember." Her voice was subdued. "But you'll be able to—"

"No, I won't. Not like I used to." The music had changed to a soft, slow number, and couples were drifting across the floor. He gestured at them, envious of their easy, light steps. "It's funny how many things I took for granted until I couldn't do them anymore."

"You can still dance. Come on, dance with me." Her voice held a stubborn ring, and he realized again that his little Sophie had grown up to be her own woman now. The thought tickled him, and he smiled down at her as she stepped in front of him and reached for his free hand, placing it at her waist.

Then the full impact of what she was doing hit him.

He couldn't believe it. He'd been wondering for days how to get her into his arms. Who'd have thought she'd be the one to initiate it? The soft flesh beneath the fabric of the black dress yielded to his gentle squeeze, and his heart began to pump double time. This close, he could smell her, the warm floral fragrance she always wore simmering in the heated crevice between her breasts, wafting up and around him every time she took a breath. No matter how many times he had held her in the past, he always marveled at how small she was. Even in the heels she wore, her eyes were barely level with his chin, and her slender shoulders looked fragile and delicate as the dim light played over her.

Her right and his left hand were already joined. While he stood, absorbing the fact that this was really happening, she raised their hands, sliding her fingers around beneath his until they were palm to palm. "There," she said. "Now you can dance."

Very slowly, she shifted her right foot forward until her weight was balanced evenly on both feet, and she began to sway back and forth. He let her push him into the same gentle rhythm, looking down into her upturned face as they moved to the music. Her eyes sparkled in the shadows, and her smile was triumphant as her eyes met his.

But the touch of her was too seductive to resist.

He slid his right hand from her waist to the sweet firm swell at the very bottom of her spine, just where her buttocks began, and pressed her tightly against him. Her head was tilted back so that she could still see his face. He could see the feminine awareness, almost panic that crept into her expression as she registered the sensual intent in his embrace. The position pushed her breasts firmly into his chest, and he had to take a deep breath and reach for self-control as he felt his body stirring, urging him to respond, to take, to make her his. To distract himself, give him time to think without those eyes assessing his every thought, he used his clasp on her other hand and drew her in, tucking her against his chest as they continued to sway. "There," he said, bending his head to her ear. "*Now* we're dancing."

She exhaled, a shaky sound that made him smile even as her hot breath raced over his throat and sent a shiver of purely sexual need skittering down his spine. "I don't think this qualifies as dancing," she said in a low, strained voice.

"Oh?" It was nice to know he wasn't the only one affected here. He nuzzled his mouth into the cloud of her dark, curly hair until he found her ear. Running his lips gently along the fragile shell to the earlobe, he sucked the tender flesh below her diamond studs into his mouth, flicking his tongue against the small hollow he discovered behind her ear. She made a little sound deep in her throat, and he felt her body loosen and melt against him. Incredibly excited by the promise inherent in her soft surrender, he put both arms around her to hold her to him, firmly pulling her into contact from neck to knee, letting her feel the hard ridge of aroused flesh he couldn't hide.

Their bodies still were swaying, barely, from side to side, and the movement of his hardness, nestled into the gently yielding curve of her belly, had him fighting a primitive urge to drag her to the floor and thrust into her again and again until he found release. Hanging on to control, he ran his mouth on down her neck to press a hot, openmouthed kiss against the warm flesh of her shoulder, noting how the skin gleamed, ivory under the pale light. "If it's not dancing, what do you call it?"

She whimpered again, and her head fell back, exposing the long, pale column of her throat to his marauding mouth as her hands clutched at his back. "A problem."

He chuckled. "There's a solution to every problem, baby." He raised his head then, looking down at her dazed expression, mouth slightly open as her breath rushed in and out, her eyes wide and clouded. "And I can fix this one." All amusement fled, and he lowered his mouth to hers.

Sweet. Warm. Yielding. Her lips had been made for kissing him, he thought, angling his head for a better fit as he traced the soft line, slipping his tongue inside her mouth

and searching out hers, enticing her into a wordless, mindless mating of their mouths that had the blood rushing to
his head and his knees practically shaking. He leaned back
against the windowsill and drew her between his knees, still
keeping her flush against him, thoroughly enjoying the way
her hips cradled his rising flesh.

He realized he was still rocking her in time to the music's
beat and he lifted his head a fraction, dragging his fingers
through her hair to cradle her skull in his hand as he reck-
lessly dropped kisses across her cheekbone, up her temple
and down her nose before coming back to the irresistible
lure of her mouth and plunging his tongue deeply, possessively, inside.

"Hey, you two." The deep, amused voice jolted them
both, and Marco lifted his head to see Sophie's oldest
brother, Stefano, standing in the opening to the little corner.
"This is a dance, remember?"

"Go away, Steffie," he said, cradling Sophie's head as
she turned her face into his shoulder. "We are dancing."

"Sheesh." Her brother's lips tilted up, and his eyes lit
with humor. "If this is what passes for dancing when a guy
has a bum leg, I think I'll try it."

"Not with my girl."

Stefano's eyes narrowed, just the slightest bit, and his
smile became a baring of teeth. "She's my sister, and I
didn't know she was your girl, Marc. You broke her heart
on your way off to God-knows-where, remember?"

He shot Stef a look that told him clearly that if he didn't
have Sophie in his arms, he'd answer another way. "I always wanted her. This time, I'm keeping her."

Sophie was squirming against him, and he relaxed the
pressure of his hand so that she could twist her head
around. "I am not a piece of furniture," she said in a furious undertone. "I don't need your protection, Steffie."

Then she turned on Marco, poking a stiff and angry finger into his chest so hard it actually hurt. "And no one gets me unless I say so."

Stef raised his hands. "All right. I was just trying to help."

"Go away!"

Stef's face relaxed; he grinned again, throwing an amused look in Marco's direction. "Yes, ma'am. Right away, ma'am." And he turned and plunged back into the crowded party room.

Before she could start again, Marco slid his hand to the back of her neck. Slowly Sophie turned to face him and leaned back in his arms, and he was struck anew by the beauty of her thick-fringed eyes beneath the silky arches of her eyebrows—although he realized those eyes were regarding him with more than a little annoyance right now.

"Sorry about that," he said ruefully. "Your brother—"

"Is as bad as you are." Sophie pushed against his chest and almost got away before he hauled her up against him again.

"I didn't mean it exactly the way it sounded," he said, trying to soothe her.

"I know." Her voice was resigned and just a little remote. "You were just doing the macho thing, you didn't really mean what you said. It's okay. We just got a little carried away."

"A little carried away," he repeated thoughtfully. "I'm not apologizing for kissing you. I'm just sorry your nosy brother interrupted us. And what makes you think I didn't mean anything by it?"

"You never did before." Her hand flew to her mouth as if she could snatch back the unguarded comment.

"Ouch." He winced. "I guess I deserved that." Then he slowly released her from his arms, holding her bare shoulders cradled in his palms as he looked down into her face. "But I do mean it this time, Sophie. I'm back and I'm staying. In Chicago, in your life. So get used to it." He dropped a quick, hard kiss on her lips and spun her around, giving her a little push back around the pillar, enjoying her wide-eyed speechlessness. "We'll finish this in a better place, at a better time."

But she wasn't quite the pushover she'd been years ago. As she turned to leave their private corner, she paused at the pillar and looked back, and her eyes were as serious as the tone of her voice. "If we finish it at all."

She must have been temporarily insane. There was no other explanation for it. Sophie tossed her dry-cleaning—including Saturday night's black dress—into her car and shot off to work on Monday morning. But the whole time, she was doing what she'd done for the rest of the weekend.

Beating herself with a big stick.

She had known, deep down, that friendship wasn't all that was on Marco's mind, from the first time she'd seen him again. She had known she was playing with fire, agreeing to go with him on what he insisted weren't dates. And she certainly had known, when he took her to the dance, that she should have had better sense than to be alone with him in a secluded place.

Her body tingled and she squirmed a little in her seat, remembering the heat that had risen the minute he'd begun to kiss her. She had no defenses against Marco Esposito, and still she had gone to him, even encouraged him with that dumb dancing idea because he'd looked so defeated, sitting there on that windowsill all alone.

Yes, she must have been insane.

But she wasn't going to give in to lunacy or misguided compassion anymore. Her heart couldn't take another bout with Marco; she'd been KO'd in the first round once and she wasn't getting back in the ring....

She went with him to the airport the next morning.

She didn't know what she'd expected after last night, but impatience mixed with brooding silence was what she got. Marco barely spoke to her as he went through preboarding rituals.

She trotted silently along beside him until they got to his gate. To her shock, his flight was already being called. She didn't know what was wrong, but she couldn't leave it this way. Not after last night.

"Are you angry with me?" she asked timidly.

Marco froze. Slowly he turned to her, and a huge sigh shook him. "No, baby," he said, taking her hand. "I'm angry with myself."

She smiled uncertainly. "Why?"

He took both her hands in his, brushing his thumbs over her knuckles as he spoke, looking at their joined hands rather than at her. "Last night was wrong. I never should have—"

"I wanted you to," she said fiercely. "Last night was wonderful. And I'm not sorry."

"But I am," he said gently. "Sophie...I'm not the kind of guy who settles down. My life is a few weeks here, a few weeks there. Mosquitoes, malaria, mudslides. It would never do for you."

"I'll wait," she said. "Marco, I love you. Please—"

"Sh-h-h." He put a finger to her lips. "I'm not talking about a year or two, baby. This is my life. You need a man who can give you security, a nice little house and a few children for your mama to spoil." He swallowed. "I'm not that man."

She couldn't prevent the tears that escaped. "You don't know that. Things could change."

He shook his head. "Not that much." He took her by the shoulders, looking into her eyes with commanding intensity. "Don't wait for me, Sophie. I won't be back again."

She was too shocked to respond. He'd used the moment to pull her against him, black flight bag already slung over his shoulder, brushing away her tears with a gentle thumb. "I have to go, baby," he said. "I should have gone yesterday."

With an incoherent cry, she flung her arms around his neck, pressing passionate kisses on him. For a moment his hands had tightened on her shoulders. He'd drawn her in and returned the kiss one last time, and then he was striding away into the tunnel toward his plane.

He'd broken her heart in two that day. Even so, she hadn't believed him. She'd waited anyway, sure he would change his mind. A year had passed. Hope had dimmed. At the end of the second year, Kirk asked her to marry him.

She'd almost refused him, but she was lonely. Kirk offered love and companionship, and finally she'd buried her dreams of Marco and moved on with her life. Only now he was back…and she found she hadn't moved very far at all.

Five

Fortunately, she was too busy during the morning to think any more about him. Her caseload was overwhelming; she simply had to fit some home visits into her schedule somewhere. Maybe after the afternoon infant care class she could slip by and visit the hospital, see the abused brother and sister for whom she was arranging foster care.

Lunchtime rolled around before she knew it. She'd been rushed because she got up late, so she hadn't packed anything for lunch. All the other staff members were eating in, but she locked her files and picked up her purse. She could run down to El Milagro, a little Mexican place that served some of the best food she'd ever had.

It was a beautiful day. The late May sun was warm and the breeze was light. As she closed the door of the Mama y Bebe Center behind her, footsteps came up the steps behind her, and she turned with a smile, ready to explain that the center closed over the noon hour except by appointment.

But the person now on the porch wasn't a client. No, the six-foot-plus single-minded Italian male could be only one thing and it wasn't a client, it was trouble. With a capital T. But it was hard to hear the warning over the sudden thundering of her heart and the roaring in her ears.

"Hola." Marco stopped before her, the devilish grin she couldn't resist quirking his lips. "Is that the appropriate greeting for this neck of the woods?"

"Sí." She nodded, determined not to act surprised. "The center is closed for lunch. If you need to see someone, we'll be open again at one."

"Then it's lucky for me the someone I need to see is standing here in front of me. Going to lunch?"

"Yes, but—"

"Great. Mind if I tag along?"

"Yes, I—"

"Okay, if you insist." He took her hand and tugged her off the porch, heading in the wrong direction from the little restaurant.

"Wait." She pulled her hand free and pointed the other way. "The place I'm going is two blocks this way."

"No problem." He reversed course and began to walk along beside her. She kept both hands in her pockets, determined not to allow him to take her hand again. Her whole body was still responding to that simple clasp of his hand from a moment ago. Her clothing felt heavy and clingy against her skin; her thighs brushed as she walked, sending awareness rushing through her.

"What are you doing here?" Attack wasn't usually the best strategy with Marco, but she couldn't believe he'd found her office and come all the way down here.

"Having lunch with you." He reached out and brushed

away a curl that was flying across her face. "I was coming to the door when you came out. Perfect timing."

"For you, maybe." They crossed the street and started down the next block. "I don't remember making lunch plans with you."

"It was an impulse decision," he said. "I went to the university library this morning to do some research for one of the classes I'm teaching over at Purdue. I thought I'd swing by here on the way home."

That distracted her. "When do you start? What are you teaching?"

"I'll be teaching a five-week environmental geology seminar through late June and July. Then I have August off and the fall semester begins after Labor Day. I drew the line at teaching more than one general studies class, so I have an intro course, a glaciology seminar and a third one on crustal and mantle dynamics."

She had to smile. "What, you don't like underclassmen?"

"Let's just say I prefer working with students who are interested in their courses," he said dryly. "And I'm not even sure I'm going to like that full-time. My teaching experience has been limited to fieldwork seminars, speeches and a few minicourses like this thing coming up in June. Teaching a class that lasts an entire sixteen weeks is going to be a whole new experience."

"You sound…less than enthusiastic."

"I'm sure I'll enjoy the students once things get started." But he sounded like he was trying to convince himself. "It's going to be different from what I used to do."

"And you wish it didn't have to be." She hadn't missed the edge in his voice, though she doubted he was even aware of it.

"Being forced out of your occupation by a physical in-

ability to make the grade isn't exactly a great feeling," he
said, shrugging. "But there's nothing I can do about it, so
there's no sense thinking about it."

Maybe not, but she suspected he thought about it a lot
more than he wanted anyone to know. "So instead, you're
down here harassing me." But she said it with a smile.

"Yeah." He chuckled. "My second-favorite occupation."

Hurt sliced through her with an unexpected ferocity that
momentarily robbed her of speech. Then she mentally
shook herself. He was not going to get the chance to hurt
her again, and she forced a teasing lightness into her voice.
"That's me—second runner-up."

There was a small, telling silence, and she knew he had
realized what he'd said. "Sophie, I didn't mean that you
aren't as important to me as my work."

The restaurant was just two doors down, and she quickened her pace, aware that he would have trouble keeping
up with the faster stride. "It's all right, Marco. Fortunately,
I stopped worrying about my place in your life plan years
ago."

She pulled open the narrow door with more force than
necessary, taking deep, calming breaths as they approached
the counter, behind which three women in black dresses
wearing hair nets buzzed around preparing food, while a
small, dark man watched every move with an eagle eye as
he made the cash register sing.

Then she turned to Marco, needing him to see how little
the conversation had affected her. "What do you think?"

He looked around slowly and she saw the familiar eatery
through his eyes. The menu and other signs were in Span-
ish, and the tiny, crowded room was scrupulously clean.
The small tables with their cheap plastic chairs sported
squat vases of faded plastic flowers and the walls were

hung with vivid oil-paint-on-velvet creations, many of which bore price tags. In a corner hung a picture of the Madonna with red and white felt roses.

"It's got...atmosphere," he said, and she was relieved to see amusement return to his eyes as he studied their surroundings. She found it unnerving when he turned the intensity of those dark eyes on her.

"Just think, that one of the matador could be yours for a modest sum."

"No," he said hastily. "It looks perfect in here. I wouldn't think of taking it." He turned and smiled down at her, but in the depths of his eyes was a seriousness that warned her the previous discussion hadn't been forgotten. "So what do you recommend, señorita?"

She considered a moment. "The *chile rellenos* are excellent." Even if the dish did tend to burn right through your stomach lining. "I'm having the *bistek*."

"That would be beef and cabbage, right?"

"Right."

"I'll try the *rellenos,*" he decided. When it was their turn to order, he stepped forward and ordered for them both before she could insist on paying for her own food. She protested, but the man at the counter looked as if he was only too happy to ignore her and deal with Marco, and she finally gave up.

"I owe you money," she said when he brought the food to the little table she'd chosen.

"We'll work something out." His words were conventional but something in the tone made her glance up sharply. He was grinning like the Cheshire cat.

It raised her hackles, and she steamed silently while they ate. She realized Marco was devouring his meal, and she couldn't resist asking, "Is it too bland for you?"

But he didn't give any indication that he was bothered

by the spicy meal. "No, it's pretty darned good. Mexican food in the States usually doesn't resemble the real thing very much, but this is almost as hot as the kind I enjoy."

Oh, well. So much for inflicting pain.

Then she realized his eyes were gleaming with suppressed laughter. "Hoping to make me suffer a little, sweetheart?"

The heck with being polite. He'd barged in on her lunch; he could listen to what she'd decided. "I don't want to do this again."

His eyebrows rose. "Eat Mexican food? I think it's pretty good."

Frustration rose. "You know what I mean. Seeing you, as a friend or a date, isn't going to work for me. I'm sorry, but—"

"Why? Because we're attracted to each other? I know I rushed you the other night. Baby, you can have all the time in the world to get to know me. I can wait until you feel comfortable again."

"It's not a matter of feeling comfortable," she protested. "Things didn't work out between us years ago and I can't imagine that they'll work any better now." She looked across the table at him, wondering how she could make him understand. "I cared for you. A lot. And you left. I had a husband I loved. And he died. I'm just not sure I can deal with another relationship, of any kind."

"So we'll take it slow, until you decide how you feel." His voice was sincere. And complacent.

Her fine dark brows drew into twin lines of annoyance. "You aren't listening to me."

"Yes, I am." He reached across the table and took her hand, carrying it to his lips. First he pressed a gentle kiss into her open palm. Then, when she drew her fingers closed defensively, he turned over her fist and kissed each knuckle across the back of her hand. When he got to the end, he started back, but this time she felt his tongue, lightly probing the sensitive flesh between her fingers as his hot breath rushed over her hand. He looked up at her over their hands, and the heat burning in his gaze seared her senses and made her aware of every inch of her feminine form. And of his equally masculine one.

Then he withdrew his mouth and carried their hands down to the table again. "I just don't agree with what you said."

"My, oh, my." A dark-haired woman in a trim business suit carrying a take-out bag fanned herself with her hand as she passed them on her way out the door. "I could feel the heat clear over here. You ever decide you don't want him, honey, you just send him my way."

"Why don't you just take him now?" Sophie muttered as the woman moved on.

Marco sat back, his dimples flashing. "See? Most women consider me a prize."

"That," she said, tossing down her napkin and rising, "is because the poor, misguided fools don't know any better."

"There you go, hurting my feelings again." He might have a damaged knee, but he still managed to reach the door and hold it open for her, then drape a hard, warm arm around her as they started down the street. "It's a good thing I have a tough hide."

They walked the rest of the way back to her office in silence. She was very aware of his tall presence at her side, his muscled arm around her, the heat of his body where it brushed hers. He made her feel small and feminine and protected. All ridiculous, all totally inappropriate for a career woman of the nineties, used to taking care of herself. She should move away. The only reason she didn't was because she didn't want to give him the satisfaction of knowing he was getting to her.

The only reason.

On the sidewalk in front of the clinic, he drew her to a halt and used the arm around her shoulders to reel her in lazily, turning her toward him until he had her body pressed against his torso, her breasts flattened against the side of his chest, with her hips almost straddling one long, firm thigh. "See you tonight," he murmured as he kissed her hair.

"Tonight?" She could barely think for the sensations charging through her, making her want to go with him right now to a dim, cool room with a big, warm bed. It drove her crazy that she couldn't say no to him with any degree of success, but another part of her was stupidly glad that he still wanted her so much.

"Tonight. Unless you have other plans. You can feed me dinner, and then I'll show you the apartment I just signed a lease on." He used his free hand to tilt her chin up and lowered his head until his mouth hovered an inch from hers. "Is it a date?"

"I—yes." She wanted that mouth, wanted to feel it moving on hers, wanted to feel him moving on her, within her, more than she'd ever wanted anything in her life. But that thought led her inevitably back to the life she'd intended to have, her life with Kirk. Stiffening her limbs, she pushed at his heavy shoulders. "No. Stop it. We're on a public street in front of my workplace."

He released her, but his dark eyes assessed her face as if he knew what battle was being fought within her. "I'll bring wine and dessert."

"No. I don't want you to come over." She was calmer now that she could think again. "Just because we're a good physical combination doesn't mean I intend to start a relationship with you, Marco.''

"A good physical combination?" His mouth kicked up at one corner while he tried to keep a straight face. "Quaint phrase. Are you trying to tell me you're as hot and bothered right now as I am? Do you know what you do to me, Sophie? How hard I get just thinking about being with you?''

She put her hand over his mouth, but was immediately sorry when he captured her wrist and held her hand there, drawing more of the secret sensual patterns in her palm with his tongue, watching her the whole time as she fought knees suddenly too weak to support her.

Somehow she found the strength to tear her hand from his mouth, to turn and stand with her back to him, arms hugging herself as she gasped for breath. Fear put out the raging blaze in her system, an intense female wariness extinguishing desire. He'd hurt her once and she knew instinctively that he would do it again. "No," she said quietly. "I do not want this, Marco.''

There was a long silence behind her. Finally, equally quietly, he said, "All right." His voice was dull, lifeless, and she turned back to see him standing with his hands in his pockets, studying the sidewalk. "I apologize for making a pest of myself. I just feel…I don't know, as if I've lost everything that made me who I am already. I didn't want to lose you, too, when I saw the chance to have the kind of relationship we should have had years ago." He put out his hand and squeezed her shoulder once, gently, before letting his hand drop again. "I'll see you around.''

"See you around." She hurried inside, not waiting to see him drive away.

For over an hour she managed to keep herself busy enough to forget about him. But the moment she sat down at the battered desk in her office, he was there in her head again, as if he'd never left.

The expression on his face as he'd accepted her edict had been weary and accepting. If she didn't know better, she'd think she had hurt him.

It was the most desperate kind of manipulation, she told herself, playing on her sympathy, and the worst part about it was that she'd already fallen for it once since he'd landed back in her life. But she knew him well enough by now to realize that there were some grains of truth contained in his words.

How would she feel in the same situation? Lost and alone. Very alone.

And she knew what that was like.

Still, she couldn't let him manipulate her.

Then the thought came to her. It was so daring, so completely out of character for her that she nearly dismissed it. But still…

Why couldn't she have a relationship with him—on her terms? Why deny herself? Life had cheated her once, and now she had nothing. She was an adult now; surely she could handle a casual relationship that included a sexual element. People did it all the time. And that probably would suit Marco far more than if she threw herself at him declaring undying love.

As long as she kept in mind that he would leave again one day, she should be able to handle it.

Before she could talk herself out of it, she reached for the phone, dialing the familiar number of his parents' home.

"Hello?" The deep voice was Marco's.

She blew out a sigh of relief that she hadn't had to speak to his folks. "Marco?"

"Sophie?" His tone sharpened.

"Yes, it's me." She rushed on. "I was thinking—maybe I was wrong—would you like to come over for dinner this evening?"

The silence on the other end of the line stretched so long that she began to wonder if the connection had been broken. Then he said, "I'd like that very much." His voice was quiet. "Did you have a time in mind?"

She took a deep breath, deliberately shutting the door on her reservations. "How does seven o'clock sound? That'll give me time to get something ready, a fast pasta, probably."

"Thank you."

"You're welcome." She smiled, glad that he couldn't see her because her lips were trembling. "See you at seven."

"Six. I'll help you with it."

"Six, then."

"See you then, beautiful." And he hung up.

Before six o'clock she was going to have to do some serious soul searching, decide how much of herself she was willing to share with Marco this time. Until he left again.

She got home in plenty of time, and she took a quick shower and washed her hair before layering and baking a vegetable lasagna that was her mother's recipe—and his mother's, too, come to think of it. Her hair was still wet by the time she'd finished tossing a salad, and she got out her hair drier and blew it for a few minutes until the roots felt less damp. It was so thick and full that it took forever to dry. She'd cut it to shoulder length the summer before her wedding and had kept it the same ever since. She studied herself in the long mirror on the back of her bathroom door as she straightened from putting the drier away.

A delicate woman with a heart-shaped face and masses

of curly black hair studied her. It was still a shock, after
more than three years, not to see the well-padded person
she'd been. She hadn't lost so much weight, less than
twenty pounds. But what she had lost, she'd lost in all the
right places. Still, she'd accepted the fact that even at this
weight, her figure resembled the Venus de Milo more than
Twiggy, and she rarely thought about it anymore.

Until now. She wanted Marco to like what he saw. He'd
called her beautiful. But then, he'd called her beautiful
years before, too. At least that was one thing she never had
to worry about with Marco. He'd known her first when she
was what her father called "pleasingly plump," and he'd
liked what he'd seen, even then.

The doorbell rang, and the woman in the mirror jumped.
Her stomach leaped and bounded wildly, and she forced
herself to take a deep breath. She knew she'd agreed to
more than a simple friendship this afternoon. And after
what had occurred between them the other evening at the
party, she couldn't pretend any longer that friendship was
all there was between them.

Exactly what it was wasn't something she'd been able to
label, though she'd worried at it all afternoon. The doorbell
rang again and she turned and walked through her condo
to the door. She opened it and met Marco's eyes, dark,
disturbing, blatantly examining her figure in the leggings
and long sweater she'd worn. He looked down her body,
and slowly back up, and she let him, simply standing there
as if waiting for his approval.

He wore black jeans and a short-sleeved black T-shirt.
The combination emphasized the tough, strong lines of his
body and turned him from a handsome, teasing man to a
devastatingly rugged, sexually compelling, untamed male...

a male who was looking at her as if she was a female in heat.

The silence stretched between them a beat too long. But when she finally remembered to open her mouth to invite him in, he stepped forward before she could even get out a hello.

His big hands spanned her waist and his face became a blur as he found her mouth with his, invading the tender depths with deep, penetrating strokes of his tongue that devastated her defenses. He pulled her against his body, and she whimpered as her hips met and recognized the growing demand of his. Her breasts pressed into him and her nipples came alive, sending heated messages down to her womb to ache and throb.

Somewhere in the heated moment, she realized she was standing on her toes, straining against him, that she had put her arms around his neck and was kissing him back with the same desperate need he was showing her.

Why had she thought this was so wrong? As long as she didn't let herself pretend that there was any element of permanence in it, everything would be fine.

She ran one hand up to comb through his silky black curls and flatten against his skull, pressing her body to his, and his hard, hot male frame pressed right back. He was solidly aroused now, and he groaned as his hands slid down to her hips, holding her in place so that he could grind the unyielding length of his erection against her.

"Wait." He tore his mouth away and held her at arm's length.

Sophie blinked, still caught in her responses to his overpowering sensuality. "What for?" she said in a teasing tone. She was seized by a longing, an urgent desire to see his body, to touch all the hard flesh that felt so wonderful

against every inch of her, and she ran her fingers from the
hollow at the base of his throat down his chest to press her
palms against the packed musculature that defined his body.
But she was unprepared for the naked surge of male hunger
that hardened his dark features into a grim mask of need.

"If you don't stop that," he said between his teeth, "I'm
going to lay you down right here in this open doorway and
tear every stitch of clothing off you. Then I'm going to
make a place for myself right here—" his hand briefly slid
down to press the plump folds between her legs and moved
away again before she could do more than draw a startled
breath "—and get inside you and make you want me as
badly as I want you." His voice was hoarse and almost
angry sounding, and the rough words frightened her a little
bit even as they thrilled her.

The only other man she'd ever been with besides Marco
was Kirk, and he'd been gentle and careful, never rough
and urgent and wild. She tensed in his grip, sliding her
hands away from him. "I do want you," she admitted, "but
I'm not ready for that."

She'd thought he might be petulant, mad at her with-
drawal, so when he chuckled as he released her, she could
only stare at him with a question in her eyes.

"You could have fooled me." He gently pushed her on
into her apartment and closed the door. "Your definition
of *ready* must have come from a different dictionary than
mine."

She reached for dignity, decided she might as well forget
it. "It's exactly this kind of behavior that makes me think
it's a mistake to be seeing you," she told him.

"Why? You like it as much as I do." He hefted the bag
and walked past her into her kitchen.

"I like ice cream, too, but I don't have it for every meal," she said, trailing after him.

"Relax." He shot her the grin that weakened her knees every time he used it. She suspected he'd practiced that expression on a lot of women in a lot of places with much the same effect. "You can have as much of me as you want without gaining a pound."

There was just no way to answer that. His words raised images better left unseen, and she hurried around the counter to find a corkscrew to open the wine bottle he withdrew from the sack. She should know better than to get into verbal games with Marco. He had the quickest brain she'd ever seen; it was rare for anyone, even in his own family, to best him.

"So what did you do the rest of the afternoon?" he asked, his eyes gleaming. He knew exactly what effect his words had had on her, darn him! He took the corkscrew from her and opened the wine with a few deft, powerful twists, though he didn't add anything else of a personal nature.

She realized he was giving her the space she needed, and she gratefully seized the opportunity while she turned to get two glasses down from the cupboard. "Remember the baby I was keeping a few weeks ago?"

He nodded, smiling. "Your baby."

"Yes." She smiled, too, though a small pang squeezed her heart, and accepted the glass of wine he offered her. "I visited her mother today. She isn't sure she wants Ana back." The memory of the conversation clouded her eyes.

"Why not?" He shook his head, as if he couldn't believe her.

"The mother is barely sixteen. She was abused by an uncle and she ran away from home when she met Ana's father. They married when she got pregnant. Her family won't take her back now, or the baby. And she's afraid if she stays with her husband he's going to harm her. Or worse, hurt Ana.''

"But can't you help her get on her feet and keep the baby?" He perched on a stool at the counter and watched her arrange spinach salad on two plates.

"Yes. That's what I do." She shrugged. "But I can't do anything unless the person wants help. She feels desperate, and afraid, and overwhelmed by the idea of caring for Ana alone."

"That's sad." He picked up his wineglass and she noticed the way his big hand cradled the fragile crystal. "I see people in desperate circumstances all the time in Third World countries." He grimaced. "I did, I mean. And I've never gotten used to seeing the poverty, the disease and malnutrition.... I know I should probably want Ana's mother to keep her, but part of me says that little girl would be better off in an adoptive home."

Sophie nodded. "Possibly. But it would be a foster care placement for a while, and given what's happened in the courts these days, a lot of people won't touch it anymore."

"Foster care." He grimaced. "If someone is willing to love and cherish a child whose own parents don't want it or haven't taken care of it, they should be allowed to adopt it. Some parents shouldn't have any rights. I'd like to take the judges who make these decisions to the slums of Brazil or the streets of India, so they can see what's happening to the children while they waste words and money and time. Having a little boy die in your arms tends to change your point of view pretty quickly."

He pulled out her chair and seated her, then sat down across from her, and the action distracted her for a moment.

The easy power in his arms was always disconcerting. She knew his life until his accident had demanded that he stay fit and strong; he might have damaged his leg, but he certainly had kept himself in good condition.

As he placed his napkin across his lap, she wondered about his last sentence. "Have you had a child die in your arms?"

The idea horrified her, and she didn't know why. She'd handled children who'd been horribly abused. But it was part of her job.

Marco nodded. "I have." He didn't elaborate. The lights in his dark eyes had disappeared, and they were shadowed and unreadable. "And you know what the worst part is? Those little kids die from simple, preventable things, like influenzas and infections and dysentery."

"You must have seen a lot of that."

"Too much." His strong lips were flat and grim. "I used to fantasize about getting those little kids out of there, bringing them home to my family. And then I realized there are just too damn many. After that, I started to think about helping the parents, to give people a chance to get out of the poverty they've known their whole lives, to learn and work—" He broke off, a smile creasing his cheeks and letting his dimples appear. "I should have studied social work with you."

"No." She smiled back, glad to see the light returning to his face. "You're one of the best in your field. I kept up with some of the articles you wrote and contributed to during your years of globe-trotting."

"I *was* one of the best," he emphasized. Then speculation crept into his expression. "So you read about me?"

"From time to time," she conceded. "Your folks were

so thrilled when something came out that had your name in it—everyone on the block had to read it."

"Oh, so it was your duty." There was a strange glint in his eye now.

"Not entirely." She shrugged, determined to keep their past exposed and unremarkable. That way, it couldn't hurt. Matter-of-factly, she smiled at him. "A girl doesn't forget her first love. I was curious."

"But you did forget me just like I said you would," he pointed out. "You got married."

Six

Why had he mentioned her marriage?

Stupid, Esposito, very stupid. He'd finally gotten through the door of her apartment—and how!—and they'd been moving along pretty well.

And then he'd reminded her of her husband.

The lights and warm humor had drained out of her face and stripped away the pretenses, and now he could see what he'd been ignoring since he'd learned Sophie had gotten married.

She was grieving. Sorrow lay pooled in her dark-lashed eyes, and her full lips drooped.

Quietly, carefully, he reached across the table and took her hand, rubbing his thumb along the backs of her knuckles. She had the softest skin.… But he didn't want to be distracted yet. "He must have been a pretty special guy, if you loved him. Tell me about him."

Her eyes widened, and he realized he'd surprised her.

"We met in college," she said in a low voice. "His name was Kirk, Kirk Morrell, and he was a farm boy from a little town below Peoria." She smiled a little. "Can you imagine me a farmer's wife?"

Although the thought of her being anyone's wife tied his gut into a small, tangled knot, he forced himself to smile back, shaking his head. "Doesn't compute."

"Well, I nearly became one. Kirk was working on his Master's degree in agriculture the year we married. We planned to go back to his family's farm outside Tiskilwa after he graduated...but he got sick."

"Sick?" Part of him hated to make her relive something that was obviously painful, part of him didn't want to hear any more, but for some strange reason he felt compelled to learn everything he could about the man who'd married Sophie.

"Cancer," she said quietly, fiddling with her fork. "He had surgery, chemo, the works, and for a while the doctors thought he was going to be all right. But then it came back again."

"You barely had a chance to enjoy a normal marriage."

"That's right," she said. "We didn't. We were married three years ago, in May, and he died a year and half after that."

"I'm sorry." And he was. Even though he couldn't help being glad that he was the one sitting across the table watching the candles she'd lit throw shadows across her cheekbones, he never would have wished her husband dead.

Her lips turned up in the slightest suggestion of a smile. "I'm sorry, too. He was a sweet man." She picked up her wineglass and sipped, then nodded at him. "So tell me about the places you've been in your travels. I've never been beyond the borders of the continental United States."

He recognized a change of direction when he heard one,

and for now, he was willing to indulge her. Besides, he wanted her to think of the future. They could forget the past, starting here and now.

They talked through the meal about more general things. He described some of the places he'd been, the things he'd done, and she told him more about all of her brothers' and sisters' lives. Her four brothers were all born within six years, and Marco was older than two and younger than the two others. He'd been close to all of them, and by the time she had taken him through their various families, including Giordono's twins, he was laughing aloud.

"Twins! Somehow I can't picture ol' G as a father, especially with twin daughters."

"Twins run in the family," she reminded him.

"Yes, but I thought they were supposed to skip a generation."

"They did," she pointed out as they carried their dishes to the kitchen. "Just leave these. I can clean them up later—where was I? Oh. Mama's mother was a twin, and Mama had twins. But G wasn't a twin, so his twins actually skipped two generations. If your theory is correct, then Vince and Belle shouldn't have twins, since they are twins."

"Which they don't, according to you."

"Right."

"This is making my brain hurt." Marco shook his head, following her to the couch, where he set down the two cups of coffee she'd handed him.

She arranged a plate of her mother's cookies on the coffee table and sank down with a wave of her hand. "Please eat those. Mama insists on sending me home after every visit loaded down with more food than I could eat in a month. I take it to work and palm it off on my co-workers, who don't need all these calories, either."

She sat down beside him, and he restrained the urge to pull her close to his side. His body wanted to finish what he had started in her doorway when he'd arrived. But he sensed she still wasn't ready to accept him in that intimate fashion, regardless of the way she responded every time he put his hands on her. There was a wall of reserve around Sophie. Nothing too noticeable unless you knew her well. And he did.

He was going to have her, there was no doubt in his mind. But he didn't want her to have second thoughts afterward, and until he knew what she was thinking behind those pleasantly blank smiles she offered, he could wait.

So he reached for one of the raisin cookies that nobody could make like Mrs. Domenico and lay his head against the back of the couch, stretching out his legs. "You haven't told me when or how you lost weight. Which, by the way, is very flattering. I liked you the way you were—a lot." He laughed when she blushed. "But the cute little butt filling out these pants is pretty appealing."

She took a sip of her coffee, lingering over it until the warm color began to recede from her cheeks, then set down the cup and settled herself next to him. "When Kirk was sick, I was really busy caring for him. I didn't think much about food or sleep, and it just kind of happened." She patted one hip gently. "Now I've decided I like me this size, so I do what it takes to stay this way."

He reached over and picked up the hand she'd just used, linking his fingers with hers. "Where did you and your husband meet?" What he really wanted to know was *When? When did you stop thinking of me?* He knew it was unfair of him to even be thinking that way. He was the one who had told her to forget him and get on with her life.

But all these years, he'd subconsciously considered Sophie to be his. He'd come home wanting things to be like they'd been before, wanting her to be the same. Still untouched, still quiet until he took her in his arms, still wildly passionate and willing to give him anything he wanted.

He realized that she hadn't answered him, and he straightened on the couch enough to put his arm around her. Not pulling her close enough to make her uncomfortable, but establishing a link, a connection, between them.

Slowly, she said, "I met him in college my freshman year. We used to study together. He asked me out again and again but I always said no."

What she'd left unsaid was the reason she'd refused. Because she'd been waiting around for him.

She went on. "But after you made me see that you and I were all wrong, that I was too young, that you were too busy traveling, there was no reason for me to refuse him."

He let the silence hang, but she didn't elaborate, and he finally was forced to say, "You must not have wasted any time getting married."

She turned her head and looked at him, and he saw a small, dark fire growing in her eyes, warning him to back off. "We started seeing each other in June after I graduated and got married two years later…a lot longer than it took me to get involved with you."

He flinched, remembering how close he'd come to taking her innocence on their very first date. But, dammit, didn't he get any credit for trying to keep his hands off her?

He wanted to know more. He wanted to know when she'd become lovers with the guy, what she'd felt when another man touched her, if she'd loved Kirk like she'd said she loved him. But there were some questions even a stupid man knew better than to ask.

"I'd like to catch the news," he said instead. "Would it be all right if I turned on your TV?"

Without another word, she leaned forward and picked up

the remote, handing it to him before sitting back down a discreet distance away.

He found the channel he wanted and tossed the remote onto the table. Then he deliberately reached for her. "I'd like to hold you," he said quietly. "Just hold you."

She threw him one startled, suspicious glance, but she didn't resist as he turned and arranged them so that he was propped sideways on the sofa with her between his legs, her back against his chest.

He slipped both arms around her and pulled her back against him, linking his fingers over her waist. After an initial moment of stiff hesitation, Sophie relaxed against him, laying her head against his shoulder and her arms atop his, with her small hands clasping his forearms.

"There," he said. "Doesn't this feel good?"

Beneath his hands, he felt her take a deep breath, then let it slowly out. "Yes," she said. "This feels good."

Good was an understatement, he thought. This was heaven. Her body was warm against him, and her back rested solidly against his groin, heating his desire for her. Beneath his hands her belly was flat, her hips narrow, but if he moved his fingers the slightest bit, the backs of his knuckles brushed against the undersides of her full breasts. He wiggled his fingers now, and was rewarded by the distinct outline of her nipples, stiffening into tight little buds beneath the light sweater she wore. He was so much bigger than she that he had a clear view of her front over her shoulder when she lay back, as she was doing now.

Then he remembered the apartment. "Oh, hell."

"What? What's wrong?" She immediately tried to sit up, but he'd already made the decision in his mind, and he controlled her easily, holding her in place until she stopped struggling.

"It's no big deal," he said. "It's just that I was going

to show you the apartment I'm thinking about renting. But we could do that tomorrow.''

He could feel her relief, and it struck him that she'd really had a moment's panic, thinking something might be seriously wrong. And he supposed he could see why. In her life, things had gone seriously wrong.

To get her to smile, he said the first thing that came into his head. ''Then again, I could just move in here with you.''

But she didn't relax. In fact, she stiffened even more. ''That's not an option.'' Her voice was cool and curt, and it irritated the hell out of him. Irritated him enough that he responded in kind, wanting to get under her skin like she'd gotten under his.

Dropping his head, he nuzzled her neck, running his lips up to capture the soft fleshy nub of her earlobe. ''Why not?'' he breathed into her ear. ''After that kiss at the door, you can't pretend anymore, sweetheart. I'm going to be in your bed, and I have a feeling one or two nights a week isn't going to cut it. It sounds like a good option to me.''

He'd expected her to struggle again, to try to free herself, but he was completely unprepared when she turned, flipping herself over in his arms violently, lying nearly full-length on him. Her breasts pushed at his chest, and her legs lay between his, the hot, waiting vee between her thighs separated from his filling, throbbing shaft by nothing more than a few thin layers of clothing.

''I'm not pretending,'' she said between her teeth. ''A little romance in this relationship would have been nice, but you've never been big on romance in the past so I don't know why I expected anything different this time.'' He was too shocked to restrain her when she moved this time. His Sophie, the one he'd dreamed of so many times over the years, had spirit, but she'd never displayed a temperamental side like this.

She climbed off him. "You want to get in my bed? In my pants?" She stood over him like a dark angel, her eyebrows drawn together in fury, her eyes no longer reminding him of a doe, but a much fiercer predator. "Fine, let's go. I'm tired of arguing about it with you." She put her hands to the hem of her sweater and with one swift tug, yanked it up and over her head.

His heart almost stopped. His heart definitely damn near almost quit right on the spot. She was beautiful. A goddess. So many times, he'd imagined her like this, but his memory hadn't come close to the reality.

Seeing her body nearly naked shouldn't be such a big deal. When they'd been together years ago, he'd touched her breasts, filled his palms with the warm, sweet mounds, sucked the small buttons of her nipples into his mouth and tongued them until they were both almost crazy. He'd seen these breasts before, but nearly always, they'd been in a car or a dark, dimly lit spot where two lovers could go a little further than propriety would allow on the doorstep.

But it was a big deal. Oh, God, it was a huge deal. She wore a lacy black bra that hugged her generous curves. Black, for God's sake! Was there anything sexier than a woman in black lace?

In the hollow at the base of her throat, her skin was smooth and creamy, never touched by the sun, slipping gently down her breastbone to slope into full globes of feminine beauty. The lace of the bra wasn't designed to hide much, and he could see rosy nipples the color of warm cherry wood thrusting forward, calling him.

Then he realized Sophie's hands had gone to the snap of her slim-fitting leggings. She tugged at the closure and with a tiny, but decisive *click,* the pants were open. He didn't intend to move, didn't even consciously think of it, but as her small fingers grasped the tab of the zipper and her defiant eyes met his, he closed his fists over her hands, preventing her from exposing even more of herself to him.

"Stop it." His tongue was all tangled up, and his mouth felt like he'd chewed up a wad of sawdust. "Dammit, Sophie, just stop it." He prevented her from tearing his hands away and maneuvered himself awkwardly off the couch. Standing, he had the advantage of size, and he pulled her against him with one hand, using the other to hold both her flailing fists behind her, pushing her body against his in such a way that the erection straining at the front of his pants was pressed firmly into her naked midriff.

"Why?" she demanded. "I thought this was what you wanted, Marco. Isn't this what you've had in mind since you saw me standing in my folks' backyard?" She blew hair out of her eyes, glaring at him. "It's what I want. Not what I want to want, but it's what I want. All I can think about is you anymore. How it feels when you put your tongue in my mouth, how I want you to touch my breasts—"

He was only human. And there was absolutely no question that she was human, a sweet-scented soft human woman who was making him so crazy he couldn't think straight. Just because it was the most effective way of shutting her up, he slammed his mouth down on hers, so violently that he felt the edge of her teeth against his lip before he thrust his tongue into the warm, welcoming depths of her mouth, groaning a little when she met him thrust for thrust and her hips echoed the heated exchange, offering him the senseless, mindless pleasure of her body.

And that was the thought that stopped him.

Senseless. Mindless.

This wasn't what he wanted. Well, it was, but not quite like this.

He tore his mouth away from hers, amazed to hear himself panting. "Sweetheart, wait. I don't want this to be a five-minute rocket that goes off so fast neither one of us has time to enjoy it."

"Too bad." She opened her mouth and he readied himself for another blast, but suddenly, she shut it again and her eyes filled with tears.

Oh, hell. Not tears. He'd sooner be tortured than watch a woman cry. Especially when he suspected he was the cause of the flood. Especially this woman. The only woman with whom he'd ever wanted to share his life.

The thought was a real shocker. It sneaked out of his subconscious and plastered itself across a great big billboard in his head, and there was no shaking it loose.

The tears were on the march now, starting down her cheeks, and her small shoulders were beginning to shake. Quickly he grabbed her sweater from the couch where it had landed and dragged it over her head. He wanted to be noble, but when those two magnificent examples of female anatomy were right under his nose, nobility went south in a hurry.

"Ah, Sophie? Sweetheart? Baby, please don't cry. I'm sorry." He bent his knees, despite the stiff discomfort in the right one, until he was eye level with her. "I'm sorry," he repeated. "I want to make love with you, not just have sex, and I want it to be special. The way you've always been special."

"Uh-huh." Her petite frame was drooping now. "So special that you could walk away and forget me in a day."

"Not forget you." He used the hem of her sweater to wipe away tears, then lowered it quickly before his body could get any fresh ideas about what was under that fabric.

"I never, ever forgot you. Even when I was miles and years away, you were always the woman who won when I was comparing women in my head."

"What women?" She sniffed, but at least the tears seemed to be drying up.

"Um, you know, other guys' wives." How come he couldn't manage a little simple comfort without putting his foot right down his throat?

"Sure." It was sarcastic, but the antagonism she'd bristled with a few moments ago was gone. "Don't tell me lies, Marco. It just makes it that much harder to believe anything you say."

That burned him up. He took her chin in one hand, not caring that it wasn't quite a gentle grip. "I don't lie. I've wanted you since the day I walked away. But it seemed like the right thing to do at the time. You were too young, our families were an added complication, I wasn't planning on settling down.... Looking back, I was damn stupid. I should have married you and dragged you along to every grubby little jungle town I went to. At least you wouldn't be able to accuse me of not wanting you."

Her nose was pink and her eyes were shiny with unshed tears. And her mouth was hanging open.

His hand on her jaw gentled and he gave her a sheepish smile. "Don't look so shocked."

She gathered herself and finally managed to speak. "You thought about marrying me?"

He nodded. "It wouldn't have been fair to you."

"I would have gone, you know."

He released her chin and released her, too, stepping back to save his sanity. "I know," he said grimly. "That's exactly why I didn't ask."

"I thought it was just a convenient excuse. I thought you really didn't want me."

"Jeez. You thought I didn't want you? Couldn't you tell what I was thinking? God, Sophie, I've never felt about another woman the way I felt—feel—about you."

"Meaning?" She spoke carefully, studying him as if he were some new species of animal that might be dangerous.

Suddenly he realized this conversation was getting way too deep. He had hardly thought about these feelings himself, and he definitely wasn't ready to share them. Abruptly, he shut his mouth. He took her hand and walked with her to the door. "Meaning that you need to think about that for a while. I'm not interested in having a quick round of sex with you. But I'm leaving now because my body is arguing loudly with my reason, and I'm not sure which one will win if I don't get out of here."

"Oh." She looked dazed.

He dropped a hard kiss on her lips but had to linger for a moment and let her tongue greet him again. When he forced himself to lift his head and fumble for the doorknob, he was breathing hard. "I'll call you tomorrow."

And when he'd shut the door of her apartment behind him, he had to lean against the wall for a minute until his knees quit shaking and his body accepted the fact that it wasn't getting what it wanted. Yet.

He had a feeling he'd leaped in over his head here, and who knew how deep the water was. But since there was no way in hell he was going to be without Sophie ever again, he'd tread water until he worked it all out.

He called her at work the next day and asked if she would have dinner with him, then look at his apartment. She nearly invited him to come over and eat at her condo, but common sense prevailed. Sparks flew too wildly when they were alone together; they were much too apt to start a fire that couldn't be quelled.

She was ready when he arrived, and they went directly to a small Chinese restaurant that had been around for years. In fact, they'd eaten here together before, she was sure. When Marco escorted her in, the sense of déjà vu was even stronger, and she turned to him.

"We came here before, didn't we?"

He was grinning as they were led to their table. "Yeah. I wanted to see if you remembered."

"The food's fantastic. I remember that."

And it was. He ordered soup and they spoke of little things until their main course arrived. When the waiter had left them, he reached across the table and took her hand, holding up the glass of rice wine in a toast. "To us," he said.

Sophie hesitated a moment before gently clinking her glass against his. "To us," she repeated, and they drank. But when she had set the glass down and picked up a fork—no way was she going to humiliate herself with chopsticks, she had informed him—he could see her thoughts turning like a carousel of horses moving incessantly up, down and around, time after time after time.

"What's on your mind?" he asked.

She paused in the act of lifting a bite to her lips, then continued, chewing slowly and swallowing the crisp vegetable before she answered him. "A week ago, there was no 'us.' Now, I feel as if you have a road map of this relationship all plotted and I'm just a passenger along for the ride."

"There was always an 'us,'" he corrected. "We just didn't have time to plan the trip until now."

She frowned. "And you've mapped out the whole route already, I presume."

"I'm not sure what that means." He eyed her warily. "Is it a crime to want to be with you?" He spread his hands. "That's all I want, Sophie. Time for us to get to know each other again."

She thought about it while she finished another bite. "Okay. Let's get to know each other. Who goes first?"

"Goes first?"

"Asking the questions," she said. "That's a normal way for two people to get to know each other."

"Seems to me we already know each other pretty well," he protested.

"Then why," she asked, "do we need time to get to know each other?"

"It was just a figure of speech," he said. "I didn't mean to open up a can of worms here. Look, since you don't like the way I've been doing things, why don't you make the moves for a while?"

"What if I don't make any?"

He grinned, and her heart skipped a beat at the primitive, piratical expression. "That's the only move that's not allowed."

She gave up. There was no getting around Marco once he'd made up his mind about something. Hadn't she learned that lesson the hard way years ago?

They finished the meal in an uneasy peace and he paid the bill, then led her back to the car in the warm spring evening. "I want you to see this apartment," he said. "I don't need a lot of space. I think it'll do."

He drove her to a set of duplexes less than five minutes from her own home. After knocking on the door of the end unit, he returned with a key and helped her out of the car. "The landlady lives here as well," he said. "Which is good, because it seems to be kept up nicely, on the outside, at least."

He led her to one of the middle units and unlocked the door, then ushered her in and relocked it behind them.

"There's a laundry room, a spare room for an office, and garage down here," he told her, showing her each area. "And the main living space is upstairs."

The place had one bedroom with a private bath, a kitchen, living room and dining room and another half bath. A brick wall with a gas fireplace and mantels on each side separated the dining and living areas, and the kitchen was efficient without being cramped.

"This is really nice," she said, as he showed her into the single bedroom. "You haven't signed a lease yet?"

"No." He was busy opening closets. "I wanted you to see it."

She peeked into the bath, then turned to smile at him. "You have my blessing, for what it's worth. Go sign the darn lease before somebody else snaps it up."

He crossed the room to grab her by the waist and dig his fingers into her ribs. "All right, smartie."

She shrieked, evading the tickling and darting to the other side of the room. "Truce, truce. You know I'm completely helpless when someone tickles me." When they were much younger, her brothers had held her down and tickled her endlessly; she had distinct memories of Marco coming to her rescue more than once.

He nodded. "I remember." Then the lightness faded from his expression, replaced by a taut, hungry look that communicated itself to her instantly as he slowly crossed the room. When he reached her, he set his hands at her waist. They were so big his fingers nearly met around her torso; she was acutely aware of how small and vulnerable she was compared to his effortless strength.

"Sophie," he said, and his voice was a growl of need. "Kiss me."

Seven

His eyes were dark and full of a wordless appeal as he held her gaze. The tension in him quivered like a finely drawn wire, and an answering excitement stirred deep in her womb. Slowly she slipped her arms up, over his wide shoulders and around to clasp the back of his neck as she lifted herself on her toes. She wasn't quite tall enough to reach his mouth; she merely rested against him with her face tilted up in invitation, and after a still, silent moment of anticipation, he lowered his head.

"Just a kiss," he murmured before his lips claimed hers.

But for her, there was no "just" anything. Once he touched her, she was his to mold and shape and use as he willed. When he parted her lips and sought her tongue, she answered eagerly, pressing herself against him as he slanted his mouth over hers, holding her head in the hollow of his shoulder and gathering her to him. His hands moved restlessly up and down her back, then widened their search, streaking over her petite frame with easy, burning familiarity.

Her whole body tingled. Her breasts drew tight and when his palm slid possessively over one full mound, she gasped at the sensations that raced through her. Everywhere he touched her, he lit small fires of arousal that all went straight to her throbbing woman's channel, leaving her panting and breathless in his arms, twisting with desire unfulfilled, arching against his stroking hands until the long, hard bulge of man pushing at her belly gave her the answer she needed, the means to end the torment.

When his mouth moved from hers to cruise along her jawline and worry at the sensitive shell of her ear, she shivered with sexual delight and pulled her hands down from their clasp at his wide shoulders. Her small fingers wedged between them, finding the buttons of his shirt and hastily unfastening them until the garment hung open to his lean waist, and she slipped her palms inside, over hot male flesh and rough curling hair, seeking out flat male nipples and rubbing small circles over them until he groaned and his fingers clenched on her flesh.

Then his hands mirrored her motions, swiftly dealing with the buttons of her blouse, discovering the bra she wore and sliding beneath her armpits and around her back to unfasten the lingerie with one smooth action. He drew off her blouse and bra and leaned back away from her, and she could see his chest rising and falling with his labored breathing as his eyes took in her feminine shape.

"God, you're beautiful." It was a whisper of a prayer as he bent his head to her shoulder and slowly, slowly began to kiss his way over her silky bare flesh, framing one breast between his thumb and index finger so that it thrust forward, and she shivered with anticipation as his mouth neared the taut crest, whimpering in frustration when he bypassed the nipple to trace a long, slow path around the fullness with his tongue.

Unable to wait, she took his head and guided it to the stiff, aching crest, pushing herself at him in invitation. And when he accepted, she cried out in mingled shock and delight as his mouth closed over her, streamers of stunning sensation racing through her and weakening her knees until she hung in his arms like a doll.

He held her to him as easily as if she really was a child's toy, cradling her in one big arm as he suckled while the other hand explored her soft feminine contours, cruising over her body as if he had never learned her curves before. He stroked and petted, gradually working his way down to the hot, aching flesh of her woman's mound, and when he finally pushed his hand between her legs and clasped the full, pouting flesh through her jeans, she jerked in unbearable pleasure.

"Easy, baby, easy," he murmured. "Let's get out of these clothes."

She had a moment's awareness of their surroundings, standing in an empty bedroom of a rental unit, but as his big, blunt fingers released fastenings and removed garments and cool air washed over her body, she ceased to notice where she was.

All she noticed, all she knew, was Marco.

When he had her bare but for the tiny triangle of her lacy panties, he stripped off his own clothing, laying his shirt on the floor and drawing her down to lie with him. Willingly, she let him push her onto her back. She couldn't take her eyes off him. For so many years, she'd dreamed of him loving her again...now that it was happening, she couldn't quite believe it was real.

She swallowed as he tossed his briefs aside, baring his

body to her gaze. She hadn't seen him before…it had been dark, and she'd been far too shy to stare, in any case.

But now…now she was staring. Black curls arrowed from his breastbone down to his groin, where a thick dark cloud of soft hair surrounded the hard man flesh that thrust from his loins. He pulled himself close against her and she could feel the hot, throbbing length against her hip. She couldn't resist the impulse to touch him as intimately as he had touched her, and she slipped her hand down over the silky black trail of curls, past his navel and down between his legs to cup the soft weight of his male sac in her palm. But it wasn't enough, and as she stroked upward, finding him full and satisfyingly firm, his body jerked against her and a shudder rolled through him.

Her small hand closed over him, learning the silky texture of his male flesh, testing his inflexible strength, and as she experimentally ran her palm from the full tip down to the joint of his body, he groaned. His hand grabbed her wrist in a clasp that wasn't entirely gentle.

"Stop," he rasped, and before she could answer, he moved over her, slowly letting her have his full weight, easing his straining erection between her legs in a snug contact that made them both gasp. He ran a hand down her hip, then slipped it to the inside of her thigh, pulling it wider and settling himself more closely. Then his hand closed over her soft flesh, and her body reacted involuntarily at the searing flesh-to-flesh contact, arching up against his hand as if to trap the teasing temptation he offered.

He sent a single finger gently searching her tender folds, rubbing small patterns of liquid heat as he steadily probed deeper until the digit was within her, but before she could move he withdrew his hand, and she felt the heavy pressure of his hard, demanding staff at the portal of her body, inexorably pushing forward.

"Open your legs more," he commanded, and she did, bending her knees and placing her heels on the floor so that she could help him. He groaned as the very tip of him penetrated her, but she was too involved in the hot, sliding wonder of his possession to wait, and she shifted her buttocks off the floor, offering him her deepest secrets, imploring him with her body to give her his in return.

He lifted himself on his elbows and looked down at her as he pressed forward, eyes blazing and hot color racing up beneath his cheekbones as he took her fully.

For a long moment there was silence. Their bodies, joined in the intimacy she'd yearned for half her life, quivered; their eyes met and held.

"I've done this in my dreams," he said in a deep, gravelly voice, "but this is better than anything in my head could ever be."

She wanted to respond, but when she opened her mouth, all that came out was a quavering sob. Her legs relaxed and his weight bore her to the floor as he cupped her face in his hands and caught the tears that rolled from the corners of her eyes with his thumbs. "Baby," he pleaded, "Sophie, baby, don't cry. I thought—I hoped this was what you wanted, that it would make you happy." He paused, and even through the overwhelming emotion roiling within her, she felt his uncertainty.

"It does," she reassured him. "It does. It's only— You left and I thought…" Another sob escaped and she stopped, pressing her lips together in frustration and humiliation.

There was a long moment of silence, and he wiped away more of her tears. He said quietly, "You thought we'd never do this again." He still didn't move within her. Then he dropped his head and sought her lips with his, kissing her sweetly, with passion but also with a new tenderness that made her heart leap.

But her body was growing impatient, and as she responded to him, the kiss quickly caught fire again, growing hotter and bolder until her hips began to rock in response. He withdrew, filled her, withdrew, and returned again, establishing a steady, ever-increasing rhythm. Instinctively she matched his pace, meeting him thrust for thrust, faster and faster, feeling a taut wire drawing to an unbearable tension within her.

And then it snapped.

Her head fell back as her body jerked wildly against him, spasms of fulfillment tightening her inner muscles around him so strongly that he gave a shout and fell into his own final moments of ecstasy, his powerful body moving hard and sure. He increased his pace to a boiling cauldron of movement, and then his back arched, pushing him to the very entrance to her womb, and she felt the hot pulses of his release as his teeth clenched and he fell heavily on her, his body slowly emptying itself as he shuddered and strained against her.

She could still feel his heart racing as they lay motionless. His chest heaved and he gulped in air. Slowly his body relaxed, increment by boneless increment, until he covered her like a living blanket. He was so much bigger and heavier than she that she couldn't get a deep breath, and she feebly pushed at his shoulders.

Immediately, he rolled over, keeping his arms tight around her so that she rolled with him, until she was sprawled over him. "Sorry," he said. "I forget how little you really are."

"It's all right." Her voice was husky with satisfied passion. She moved to sit up and slide to his side, but the muscles in his arms tightened, holding her in place.

"Don't move." He pressed her head to his shoulder and tears pricked at the backs of her eyes again when she felt him press a kiss into her hair. "I want to stay like this forever."

The sentiment was so exactly her own that she started in surprise. Then she realized that while she might want to stay next to his heart for the rest of her life, Marco merely was referring to the fit of their bodies. The pain that shot through her was stunning.

She lay atop him, his body still sheathed within her, and she faced the unbearable truth. She still loved Marco. Still loved him as much, no, even more than she had when he'd held her heart in his hand years before.

And he still desired her.

Not loved, but desired.

His voice beneath her ear was a welcome distraction from the devastating realization that this man, and none other, would ever claim her heart.

"Are you thinking what I'm thinking?"

"I don't know," she replied cautiously. Her emotions couldn't stand a dissection right now, she thought dully.

"I wasn't thinking, that's what I'm thinking," Marco said, and the grim note in his voice brought her head up so that she was staring down at him.

"What?"

"Birth control." He threaded his fingers through her hair and held her face between his hands. "I didn't use any birth control." He closed his eyes and shook his head wryly, then opened them and speared her with his sharp gaze. "For the first time in my entire life, I never gave it a thought."

"It's all right—"

"No, it's not," he said sharply. "I have no intention of getting you knocked up. At least, not until after—"

"Marco." Her palm over his lips sealed off the rest of what he was going to say. "It's not the right time."

"Oh." He thought about that for a moment. "Are you sure?" When she nodded, he said, "Well, anyway, that's good. For now. Tomorrow I'll take care of getting protection."

She didn't answer as she lay her head down on his shoulder. In truth, she barely registered his words. Knives of despair sliced at her insides.

She'd accepted the reality of this relationship, recognized the limitations. Marco might say he was staying, but she knew him too well. He'd be chafing at the bit if he were tied in one place very long. Right now he'd convinced himself his traveling days were done, but she knew that wouldn't last.

He'd go away again. And, just like last time, he'd choose to go alone. No matter what he said now, she knew him too well. If this time, a night, a week or a few months, was all she could have, then she'd take it. Kirk's death had taught her how fleeting life could be. She didn't want to wake up one day and realize she'd wasted whatever time she could have had with Marco.

His hands stroking up and down her back brought her back to the present. "As much as I like this position, I think a bed would be a little more comfortable. How about if we go back to your place?"

She lifted her head and summoned a smile, setting aside her melancholy thoughts. There would be plenty of time for them someday, she was sure. "Sounds like a plan I can endorse."

Reluctantly he lifted her off him, and they rose and dressed, laughing. As they retrieved their scattered clothing, he said, "I guess I have to rent this place now that we've christened it." He returned the key to the landlady, then drove back to her condo in a comfortable silence, holding her hand lightly between them on the seat.

But as he drove, his thumb stroked sweet circles around her palm, and between her thighs, the damp, slightly tender flesh began to throb. It had always been like this with him. She'd lived in a state of permanent sexual excitement when Marco was near.

She glanced across the seat at him and caught him watching her through narrowed eyes. Her breath began to come faster and her body relaxed; her limbs felt sluggish and heavy. Slowly he lifted their joined hands and brushed them lightly over the sensitive tip of one breast, and she sucked in a surprised gasp as her whole body reacted to his sly teasing.

He chuckled. Then he opened his door and she realized they were in the parking lot in front of her building.

He hurried her out of the car and into her condo, slamming the door behind him and reaching for her the instant they were over the threshold. Drawing her against him, he immediately took her lips, his body reacting as if he hadn't just had her naked and willing beneath him thirty minutes ago.

He wanted her out of those clothes for good, and he made it so, leaving a trail of garments strewn through her apartment as he urged her toward the bedroom. She helped him willingly, and he was rocked anew by the unrestrained passion he sensed in her, by the sensual way she arched and writhed beneath his hands when he stroked over her pretty, silky flesh and tongued the hard points of her nipples.

As he stripped off his shirt, her hands were in the way, and he nearly tripped as they both struggled with his trousers. He could hear her breathing hard, knew it matched the harsh rhythms of his own respiration. She slipped her palms inside his briefs and he groaned as she pulled the fabric away from his taut, throbbing length and replaced it with her hands. His control was slipping, and his hips urgently thrust between her warm palms as she caressed him until he knew that one more stroke would end it on the spot.

It was still too new. Maybe in about a hundred years, when he didn't want her so badly, he'd be able to wait and let her play, explore him as she wished, but right now his body was issuing commands that he couldn't ignore. Sweeping an arm beneath her back and the other behind her knees, he lifted her into his arms.

"Marco! Put me down. Your knee..." She struggled frantically, and he had to lean against the wall, bare-assed and stiff as a pole, gripping her tightly and hoping like hell he didn't lose his balance.

"My knee," he said through gritted teeth, "is the least bothered part of me right now. Quit squirming and point toward the bedroom."

She giggled and stilled immediately, putting one arm around his neck and pointing back toward the little hallway. "That way. First door on the left."

Thank God it wasn't far. He was limping at the unaccustomed weight, knew she must feel it, but he'd be damned if he'd put her down now.

At the door of her bedroom he paused, seized by a jealous possessiveness that didn't surprise him. He had to know. "Did you ever share this bed?"

Fortunately he didn't have to be more specific. She knew what he was asking. "No," she said, turning her head to kiss his shoulder. "I bought this condo after—afterward, and refurnished it."

"Shh." He dropped his head and sought her lips, replacing passion with a sweet comforting kiss. "I'm sorry. It was a dumb thing to ask."

"No, it wasn't." She still had her arms around his neck, her face only inches from his. "I want this to be new, too...a new time in each of our lives."

He made it to the bed and turned, sitting down with her in his lap. He hoped she hadn't noticed how his leg was trembling. But right now his leg was the least of his concerns. Other parts of him were taking full priority.

Slowly he lifted her, turning her toward him, and she caught on right away, spreading her legs to drape over either side of his hips. He knew she probably was a little sore, but she was as frantic as he, willingly letting him pull her down onto his engorged flesh, pressing wild little kisses over his chest and shoulders as he impaled her on his aching erection and thrust strongly up to embed himself deeply with her.

"Take me," he muttered. She was incredibly snug and tight around him, her warm channel wet and slick from his recent use, and when she pushed at his shoulders, he let her lay him back so that he was lying on the bed with her astride his body. She threw her head back as her hips began to move, and he put his hands up to catch her full breasts in his big palms, roughly thumbing her nipples until they stood up in response.

But she was riding him hard, fast, frantically, and the sweet friction was mounting. Between his legs he could feel himself drawing into a taut knot of anticipation, tension pulling him into a desperate arch beneath her on the bed until, with a guttural sound that was part unbearable pleasure, part exquisite pain, he poured himself into her for the second time, overwhelmed by the unexpected bonus of unfettered, uncovered flesh—oh, hell! Protection!

But his body was galloping full out toward satisfaction,

and the thought was lost. As he climaxed, he reached between their bodies and pressed relentlessly against the swollen bud he found hiding beneath her ebony curls, and she convulsed over him immediately, her body violently jerking and rolling in huge waves of rhythmic release, her inner muscles tugging at his shaft so that they shuddered and clung together, heaving in the throes of passion until she collapsed against him.

He was so spent that he couldn't even lift his arms to embrace her. He released a great sigh, and she crawled off him to sprawl against his side, her head flopping onto his upper arm.

For a long, long time, they simply lay there, too limp and drained to move. Their bodies cooled and their breathing steadied.

When he'd regained a small flicker of energy, he said, "I thought I remembered what it was like with you, but I was wrong."

He felt her face shift against him as she smiled, and she turned her head and caught the flesh at the ball of his shoulder in a gentle bite. "I know."

For some reason the words made him feel defensive. "I was doing what I thought was best for you."

There was an instant of charged silence, and then she shrugged. "You were wrong about that, too."

The afterglow in which he'd been basking vanished abruptly. Suddenly he had an all-too-vivid image of Sophie allowing some other man to touch her the way he had. Sitting up, he shoved himself from the bed and headed for her bathroom, where he used the brief moments to get a firm grip on the fury that blasted through him, pulling his hands into impotent fists at the thought of another man teaching her about making love.

She was his, dammit! She'd always been his, and he

should have been the one. The fact that he'd walked away because he'd thought it was the right thing to do wasn't a whole hell of a lot of consolation right now.

When he returned to the bedroom, she had donned an oversize T-shirt. She turned, and in her heart-shaped face he saw uncertainty. "Would you like something to drink?" she asked.

It was a polite, neutral question that demanded a polite, neutral response. One he didn't have. "No."

Her eyes widened at the curt tone.

He walked to the side of the bed and flipped back the covers, then grabbed her hand and dragged her onto the mattress, stripping off the shirt with impatient hands until she was bare again. Reaching down, he flipped up the sheets to cover them, then drew her into his arms with her head on his shoulder. "I want," he said, "to hold you. I want to sleep with you in my arms. Do you have a problem with that?"

She lifted a hand and gently ruffled the thick hair that covered his forearm where it lay across her body. "No," she said, and there was a warm, satisfied lilt in her voice now. "I have no problem with that whatsoever."

In the middle of the night he woke, and this time he did want a drink. Sophie was sleeping soundly, still in his arms, and he carefully shifted her to the mattress, then rose and went to the kitchen, where he knocked back sixteen ounces of ice water. He carried a second full glass back to the bedroom, grabbing a coaster from the living room on the way, and set the water on the table beside the bed, then climbed back into the bed and reached for Sophie again.

When she turned into his arms, he realized she was awake, and without really thinking about it, his arms tightened possessively. "Sorry if I woke you."

"It's all right." She snuggled more fully into his embrace.

It was a good feeling. A damned good feeling. He'd never slept—in the literal sense—with a woman in his arms before. He rarely even had slept with one in his bed. His bedroom encounters weren't geared toward slumber, and on those few occasions when he had spent the night somewhere, he'd never slept well. It was even worse when a woman had stayed all night with him. The rustle and shift of another body in the bed was unsettling; he wound up hugging his side of the mattress, trying to avoid contact and wondering if it would be too rude to ask her to go the hell home.

But with Sophie...sleeping with her all cuddled up in his arms felt right.

Maybe he was just getting older. Or maybe it was because he knew he had to start thinking about settling down. That made the most sense. With Sophie, the sex was fantastic. More than fantastic. And they were comfortable together, probably because they'd grown up side by side and had been in each other's lives forever. With little effort he could imagine a lifetime of making love with her, of sleeping with her in his arms every night and waking there every morning.

He was going to marry her. He'd already decided that. Marry her and get her pregnant as fast as possible. Fill the house they were going to buy with lots of little noise-making midgets who would keep him too busy to think about why he'd had to settle down in the first place.

"What are you thinking about?" Her soft, husky voice interrupted his thoughts.

He wasn't quite ready to share what was going on in his head, but there was something else he wanted to get settled between them.

"I guess there's no need to sign the lease on that place I showed you." He ran a hand idly up and down her spine, his long fingers kneading her flesh.

"There's not?"

"No." He continued to stroke her body as if he hadn't noticed the subtle tension that stiffened her body. "Now that we're sleeping together, it would be silly for me to get a separate place."

"You want to move in here?" There was a distinctly wary tone in her voice that he didn't trust, but he forced himself to sound lazily amused, as if they were just having a casual conversation.

"You're catching on."

She didn't move, but in the dark room he sensed her withdrawing as completely as if she'd left the bed. "I don't think that's such a good idea."

"I do." He couldn't prevent the confused irritation he felt from seeping into his tone. "What's the matter with the idea?"

She took a long moment to give herself time to frame her words. "I'm not ready to share my personal space with anyone," she said.

"I'm not 'anyone,'" he pointed out, an edge in his voice.

"No," she agreed, "you're not." She lifted the hand that lay across her belly and kissed the tip of one finger. "You're...very special to me. You know that. But I've just gotten used to living alone, and I'm not ready to change that."

Well, it was going to change. And there was no point in letting her think otherwise, though he was willing to give her a little time to get used to the idea. "All right," he said in as mild a voice as he could manage. "But don't get too used to it, baby, because we're getting married before this year is over."

She sat up, twisting to look down at him in blank astonishment. "Married!"

He grinned. "I told you I was staying in your life." Taking her arm, he tugged her back into his arms.

She came willingly, but her face was still a study in shock. "I know what you said," she told him quietly. "But I didn't think you meant it."

"I meant it," he said, more grimly than he intended. "I let you get away from me once—"

"You were the one who went away," she reminded him.

"And you're never going to let me forget it, are you?" He was all too aware that she hadn't responded in an enthusiastic manner to his declaration.

She smiled at his grumpy tone. "Probably not."

"Well, it doesn't matter. You can remind me about it for the rest of our lives. You can tell our grandchildren someday if you want."

A tremor rippled through her. He couldn't miss it, as closely as he was holding her, and she didn't say anything for so long that he got worried. "Sophie?"

"Let's not rush into things," she said in a strained voice. "Can't we just take it a day at a time?"

He wanted to press her for more of a commitment. Hell, he wanted her to agree to marry him tomorrow. But she sounded so shaky and vulnerable that he couldn't bring himself to distress her more. "All right," he said. "We have lots of days ahead of us to make decisions."

She turned to him then, sliding her arms around his neck, and her bare body shifted against his, arousing within him the desire that had been temporarily slaked. He stroked his hand over her silky skin to her hip, pulling her against him. As he rolled atop her, he had a moment's astonishment at his body's stamina. He should be exhausted. Especially the part of him that was coming vigorously alive and hungry for more of Sophie's soft flesh.

Her legs parted and she made a low hum of approval as he settled himself between her thighs. He slid into her in one long, smooth stroke as he dropped his head and sought her lips. And as he began to move within her, he decided that if he had to make a life-style change, this was probably the very best option he could have chosen. No sense in thinking about what would never be. No, he'd make the most of what he'd been offered, a woman whose mere presence could lighten the cloud of despair that had woken with him his first day in the hospital in Rio.

Eight

He was with her every moment that she wasn't working, for the rest of the week, except for the hour in the morning when he swam. Every moment. At the breakfast table, in the shower, at lunch, over dinner, and in her bed every single night.

His first class at Purdue started during June, and he had two weeks yet before the first day. Already he was driving to and from the university, doing research and preparing for the courses on a daily basis but he came over every evening when she returned from work, and he didn't leave again until she did in the morning.

Sophie floated to and from work in a sensual daze, too content even to blush when her co-workers teased her after one of them caught her locked in Marco's arms on the front stoop of the center one day.

Was she being silly, refusing to let him move in with her? She pondered the question one afternoon as she changed from the clothes she'd worn to work into a short skirt in vivid aqua and a matching top, then went to the kitchen to start some dinner. Marco was still over at Purdue, but he should be home any minute—he should be home. It was a shock to realize she already felt as if they were sharing a home, and she wasn't sure she liked it.

He was spending every moment there now, and she'd noticed he'd appropriated part of a drawer and a shelf in her bathroom cabinet. He had told her she had time to think about marrying him, but she'd seen Marco in action before. Once he'd decided on a plan, he quietly went about making it happen, regardless of what stood in his way.

It was a little scary to realize that she was part of his plan this time.

A little unnerving, and yet flattering. Exhilarating, and yet...

And yet...if she was honest, her feelings were a strange mixture of intense delight mixed with a sense of...what? Resentment, she supposed. A little part of her resented the fact that Marco had come home expecting her to fall into his arms and his plans.

She had been available in the past when he showed up, and she supposed it wasn't unreasonable of him to hope that she'd still be available. But it almost was as if he'd known she'd be waiting. What if she'd still been married? What if Kirk hadn't died? What would have happened then? Would Marco have simply shrugged and walked away?

She was afraid she knew the answer. And it told her that he could never care for her in the all-consuming way that she loved him.

His key scraping in the lock gave her an instant's warning before the door swung open and she caught her breath as he appeared. He filled the doorway, bigger always than she imagined him, and the corners of his lips slid up into the roguish grin that melted her insides and weakened her legs.

He shut the door behind him. "Hi."

"Hi." She still couldn't breathe as he walked across the room, and when he took her by the hips and pulled her against him, she knew by the sharp, hungry look in his eyes that he wasn't oblivious to her body's reaction to him.

But then his eyes narrowed, and he took her by the arms, holding her away from him. "What's wrong? Have a bad day?"

She was startled, and panicked by his perceptiveness. "No—I—uh, nothing's wrong." Inspiration seized her. "I missed you today."

"I missed you, too," he said, bending his head to take her mouth in a deep, masterful kiss that reestablished his claim. He bent her backward over his arm and stroked a hand down over the line of her throat, tracing her collarbone and trailing down across the fine flesh revealed by her V-necked top until his palm slipped onto the full mound of her breast and his teasing fingers coaxed her nipple into a taut little button of sensation, making her gasp and clench her fingers in his hair. He caressed her for another minute before slowly easing her upright, gentling the kiss and finally lifting his head from hers.

"Welcome home," she managed, leaning back in his embrace to survey his face. She deliberately thrust the unhappy thoughts of a moment before back into hiding and offered him a smile. "Are you hungry?"

He grinned and his eyes glittered. "Yeah. I'm hungry. I'm starving."

"Not for that. I was talking about dinner."

"Oh." His face fell into exaggerated lines of discontent. "You meant food."

She nodded. "Sustenance. Fuel. You know, that stuff that keeps us from dying."

"I'm dying anyway." He made a production of glancing at his watch. "It's been almost nineteen hours since—"

Sophie put her hand over his mouth. "You're terrible. Don't you think of anything but sex?"

"Nope." He took her hand and began to press lazy kisses into her palm, stroking his tongue across her flesh, working his way up over her wrist to the tender flesh inside her elbow, and she shuddered in an uncontrollable, elementary response to his sensual persuasion. "I think about you all day long, about the little noise you make in your throat when I touch your breast, about how silky the skin feels right at the top of your inner thighs, about the way you dig in your heels and arch your back—"

"Stop." She buried her face in his chest, ridiculously embarrassed.

"Why?" But he took pity on her and led her over to the sofa. "Sit down here and tell me about your day."

She allowed him to pull her down beside him, and he stretched his long legs out, keeping one arm firmly around her while she told him about the parenting class she was teaching for fathers at the clinic. Then she remembered something.

"How was your day? Didn't you have a doctor's appointment?"

He shrugged. "It was fine."

He'd stiffened when she mentioned the doctor. She hadn't imagined it. And his tone of voice definitely indicated the subject wasn't one he wanted to pursue. Fear clutched at her heart. "Is everything all right? What did he say?"

Agitation sharpened her own tone and she sat up, struggling free of his arm and turning to survey him. He looked fine, but that was no indicator of his health, she knew from bitter experience.

"Everything's fine," he repeated.

Marco never complained. Never expressed disappointment, sadness, anger. On the surface he appeared to be completely at peace with the sweeping changes the accident had forced into his life. But she knew him too well. He wasn't as unaffected as he wanted the world to believe. She waited, but he didn't say anything more.

There was an awkward silence. Something was wrong—she knew it—and his refusal to share his problems with her reminded her forcefully of the way he'd treated her when she'd been a young woman in love with him six years ago. The agony of his departures returned, and she realized that while he might be here with her physically, there was still an insurmountable wall between them. A wall behind which the real Marco Esposito hid his fears and his feelings, a wall he'd never let her scale.

Silently she rose from the couch and started for the kitchen.

"Where are you going?"

"I have to set the table," she said tonelessly.

"Wait." He caught her wrist and tugged her back to the seat. He hesitated for a moment, and despite herself, her heart rose hopefully.

"Tomorrow, two friends of mine are coming through town."

"That's nice." She averted her face so that he wouldn't see the disappointment she couldn't hide.

"Sophie…" He sighed heavily. "The doctor's appointment really was fine. I keep dreaming he'll tell me I'm doing better than he'd ever imagined, and that he'll pronounce me a medical miracle, that I'll make a full recovery."

"Oh, Marco." She reached for him, but he caught her hands in his and gave a laughing half shrug.

"One of these days, I'll get used to being a cripple."

"You are not a cripple," she said vehemently. "That's an awful word and I don't want to hear it again."

"Yes, ma'am." The corners of his eyes crinkled. "Never again, ma'am."

Though he was smiling, there still were shadows buried deep in his soul. She could see them, but it was clear that he didn't intend to tell her anything more.

Forcing back the hurt, she said, "So tell me about these friends of yours."

"All right. They're both scientists. They have a little girl. And they're two of my favorite people in the whole world, outside my family. I'm counting on you to help me entertain them."

She knew it was stupid to be pleased about such a little thing, but she was thrilled. He wanted her to meet his friends!

"There they are. J.V.! Merry!" The next day, Marco lifted his hand and Sophie watched as two of the tallest people she'd ever seen altered course and strode toward them through O'Hare, Chicago's biggest and busiest airport.

The man was a red-headed giant with shoulders as wide as her parents' house and a neat red beard. Beside him, the tall, slim woman with the white-blond hair looked almost petite.

Until she stepped forward and hugged Marco, and Sophie realized that Meredith Bayliss-Adamson was only a scant inch shorter than Marco, even in the flat sandals she wore.

She was carrying a toddler with a cloud of red-gold curls, and the little girl shrank back in shy flirtation, clutching her mother's braid to her cheek and smiling around the thumb in her mouth while she regarded the strangers with wide eyes as blue as her mother's. Marco released the woman, laughing as he touched the little one's nose with a gentle finger.

"You don't know me, do you, sweet thing?"

"This is your godfather, Kitty," her mother said.

"But don't listen to a thing he tells you," cautioned her father. Jared Adamson came toward his friend, arms outstretched, and dragged Marco into a bear hug that looked as if he intended to crack some ribs. But instead of the back-slapping he-man ritual that Sophie expected, there was a tense moment of total silence. Jared's fingers were white where they gripped Marco's back; his eyes were squeezed tightly closed.

Sophie felt tears rise and begin to burn behind her own eyes at the naked emotion on the bigger man's face. And though she couldn't see Marco's expression, she suspected it was much the same.

"You scared the living hell out of me, buddy." Jared's voice was hoarse, but he grinned as he stepped back. "You look a lot better than you did the last time I saw you."

"Thanks to you."

Jared brushed that aside. "It's really good to see you. How's the leg?"

"Good, good, can't complain."

Did she imagine it or had Marco's shoulders tensed? Jared didn't appear to notice anything. But his wife's expression registered a quiet concern that Sophie knew all too well.

"And I want you to meet Sophie." Marco put his arm around her waist and drew her forward. "Sophie, this is my esteemed colleague, Dr. Jared Vanner-Adamson, and his far-too-good-for-him wife, Dr. Meredith Bayliss-

Adamson. And the little charmer is my godchild, Katherine, but she answers to Kitty. Jared, Merry, this is Sophie.''

"It's nice to meet you, Sophie." Merry offered her a warm smile as she took Sophie's hand in a friendly grip.

Jared's eyes were molten gold, alive with speculation as he took her hand in one immense palm while he looked her over. "Hello, Sophie. I want to know why you're hanging out with a shady character like this one. But first, is there a last name that goes with 'Sophie'?''

She smiled at the big man, liking the open friendliness in his gaze. But before she could reply, Marco pulled her closer in an open display of affection. "There is, but you don't need to know it. Soon she'll be Sophia Esposito.''

The conversation stopped.

Around them, the noises of other travelers and the midday hustle of the airport suddenly seemed loud and intrusive. Jared's eyebrows rose practically to his hairline and Merry's eyes were wide with surprise.

Marco reached out and pressed a not-so-gentle fist to his large friend's lower jaw. "Shut your mouth, old man. You're attracting flies.''

She could feel a blush working its way up her cheeks, and she didn't know what to say to his friends' obvious stupefaction. But she did know she couldn't let Marco railroad her into a wedding, or even an engagement, without taking a stand. So she turned to Jared and Merry Adamson and tapped a finger against her temple in a gesture that clearly questioned Marco's sanity.

"I have no plans to change my name or my marital status,'' she said in a firm voice, extending her hand to Merry when Jared released it. "I'm Sophie Morrell and it's a pleasure to meet all of you. Marco's seven years older than me, and sometimes I think he's getting a little senile.''

She turned to Marco with a gentle smile and pinched his cheek. "But I humor him."

Jared began to laugh, his booming voice attracting curious glances from travelers around them. "This one's got your number," he informed Marco with great satisfaction.

Marco glowered, but she could tell he wasn't really annoyed. Then his expression softened. "She can have anything of mine she wants," he said, holding her gaze, "but she's not getting rid of me."

There was a short, awkward silence as she pondered what to say to that. Jared's eyebrows rose higher and his grin broadened even more.

Before he could speak, she rushed to fill the gap. "You must be tired. The car's parked in the short-term lot. We'll get your luggage and take you to Marco's condo."

"We don't want to put you out," Merry said to Marco as they headed through the terminal to Baggage Claim. "We can stay in a hotel—"

"You're staying at my place," Marco said. "There's plenty of room. I spend most of my time at Sophie's, anyway, so you'll have it to yourselves."

She felt the blush returning, and she stifled the urge to kick him in the shins as they waited for the bags to appear. Marco seemed determined to announce to the world that she belonged to him in every way there was. She was sure his friends had no illusions about why they would have his place to themselves.

She was quiet during the ride to Marco's condo, but the other three didn't appear to notice as they caught up on the mutual friends they had and Jared shared information on their recent expedition in the African veld. Little Kitty had been only three months old when they took the assignment, Merry explained, and the experience had had its interesting moments.

They arrived at the condo shortly after that, and while Marco and Jared were unloading suitcases from the trunk, Sophie slid across to the driver's seat. After all, it was her car they had been driving.

"Hey," Marco said. "Where do you think you're going?"

"Home," she replied firmly, avoiding his searching gaze. "You and your friends have some catching up to do. Why don't you spend the afternoon with them and then all of you can come to my place for dinner tonight?"

"I thought we'd take them downtown for dinner." Marco was frowning.

"Actually, we'd probably enjoy dinner at Sophie's more," Merry said from behind him. "If it isn't an imposition, Sophie. Eating out with a jet-lagged toddler might be a recipe for The Meal From Hell."

"It's no trouble," Sophie assured her. "I'll plan the meal for six-thirty. That should give you plenty of time to rest and relax."

"Wonderful! See you then." Merry turned away, following her husband up the sidewalk, but Marco lingered for a moment. His face had almost a grim set to it, and she wondered what was the matter. But before she could ask, he said in a clipped voice, "All right. Since you girls have already made plans, we'll see you at six-thirty."

There was nothing more to say, apparently, because without so much as a peck on the cheek, he turned and followed his guests.

She prepared veal scallopini, figuring that Jared and Merry would enjoy a glimpse of Marco's Italian heritage. Then she gave the apartment a quick cleanup, although she normally kept it spotless, anyway, and changed into a casual skirt and matching tunic sweater in melon before setting the table. She took the precaution of placing breakable things high out of Kitty's reach and got out a supply of toys that she kept for her nieces and nephews.

It was the first thing Merry noticed when she showed them into the apartment. "I hope you didn't go to any trouble for us," she exclaimed.

"I didn't, I swear." Sophie was amused. "I'm the youngest of seven, and most of my brothers and sisters have children. I've acquired a lot of toys over the years."

"We really appreciate you taking time to entertain us," Merry said. "We had expected to grab a quick visit with Marco, but this is so much better."

"No problem." Marco spoke before Sophie could answer her. "It's not like I have a lot to do with my time these days." The comment was surprisingly caustic. Then, as if he realized how he'd sounded, he grinned. "I'm a man of leisure now. No more leeches and mosquitoes to contend with—just students."

Perhaps she only imagined that the grin looked forced and sick around the edges.

Over dinner the talk was largely of old expeditions. Jared and Marco had worked together more than a dozen times, and each time one man told a story, the other invariably topped it with something even more outrageous. Several times she caught an odd expression on Marco's face, and though she couldn't say why, she had the strongest urge to offer him comfort. Once she reached for his hand and linked her fingers with his, and the pressure in the grip he returned was enough to make her hide a wince. She didn't think he even realized it.

She heard about the time Jared and Marco got stranded in the jungle when a rope bridge across a ravine broke ahead of them. They talked about being stuck inside a tiny tent for ten days in a windstorm, of being confronted by jungle natives carrying blowpipes with darts tipped with curare, and of their canoe overturning and dumping the two men into a river full of aggressive hippos and piranhas. Marco teased Jared about his initial annoyance six years ago when he'd realized the man he'd selected for a Venezuelan exploration was actually a woman—namely Merry—and they reminisced about expeditions the three of them had done together since then.

"So where are you off to next?" Marco threw out the question as the four of them relaxed over coffee in Sophie's living room after the meal. Kitty had played until her little eyes closed and Merry had laid her in the crib in Sophie's spare room.

Jared and Merry glanced at each other, a private exchange that was so intimate Sophie felt like an intruder for witnessing it. "Hawaii," Jared said. He placed an arm around his wife and lightly caressed her upper arm with his fingers.

"Hawaii? What's going on in Hawaii that's so exciting you two want to be in on it?" Marco sounded utterly perplexed, and Sophie deduced from his tone that Hawaii wasn't an answer he'd expected.

Merry laughed. "In terms of our work, nothing earth-shattering. Jared's going to be teaching at the University of Hawaii and I'll continue to research and illustrate native flora. I already have a contract for another textbook."

"In terms of our family…" Jared smiled down at his wife again, and Sophie caught her breath at the love in his gaze. "Now that is earth-shattering. We're going to have another baby."

Sophie forced herself to smile. "Congratulations!" Jealousy was an unbecoming emotion. She regretted still that she hadn't been able to get pregnant before Kirk died. Now…she couldn't allow herself to believe that children with Marco were in her future.

"Hey, that's great. But—" Marco lifted his shoulders in an uncomprehending shrug. "Isn't that going to be kind of...boring? If you'll excuse me for being blunt."

Jared grinned. "Spoken by a true bachelor. No, my friend, I sincerely doubt we'll have time to be bored. Just keeping up with Kitty takes both of us. Managing two is going to prepare me for sainthood."

"But what about expeditions?" There was an odd note in Marco's voice, almost one of panic. She wondered what in the world he was thinking.

"We'd still like to do fieldwork occasionally," said Merry. "In fact, if I had my way, we wouldn't be settling into one place at all—"

"But I refuse to drag two little kids all over the globe," her husband said. "They'll be older in a few years. We can decide then what we want to do. Hawaii was our compromise."

Marco was shaking his head. "Unbelievable. If I wasn't hearing this with my own ears, I'd call anyone who tried to sell it to me a liar."

Merry laughed. "That's exactly what I said when he ran it by me the first time! But he promised me we wouldn't give up fieldwork forever, so I figured I could survive civilization for a few years." She yawned, then turned to her husband. "I hate to break up the get-together, but I'm exhausted."

"I'm tired, too." Jared turned to Marco. "I'd like to talk all night, but our flight goes out at noon tomorrow, and we need to get some rest before the next leg of the trip."

Sophie rose and began to gather coffee cups. "It's been lovely meeting you both. Marco will drive you back to his place."

Merry stood as well. "Here, let me help you clean up before we leave."

"No, no, I'll get it."

But Merry was already following her to the kitchen with two hands filled with dishes. As Sophie opened the dishwasher and began to place the plates inside, Merry said, "I hope you and Marco will be happy together, Sophie."

Sophie straightened, turning to look at the taller woman. "Thanks, but Marco and I are just enjoying each other's company. As for what the future holds, I'd be afraid to even take a guess." She shrugged and tried for a wry smile. "I've had enough experience with Marco to be sure that whatever I thought was going to happen is probably the last thing that really occurs."

"You've known him for a long time, then?"

"Years and years." Slowly she reached for another dish.

"You must know him well. How is he really doing now?" Merry asked in a low tone. "Jared's been terribly worried about him ever since—well, we chose this route more because we wanted to see him than because we wanted to come through O'Hare Airport."

Sophie put down the cup she was holding. She looked at Merry and lifted her hands helplessly. "I can't tell you, because I don't know. He pretends everything is fine, but sometimes I know it isn't. But he doesn't let me—or anyone else—close enough to find out what's wrong." The words hurt when she uttered them aloud, she discovered.

Merry's eyes softened in sympathy. "There's a deep, complex personality under that laid-back exterior he hides behind, isn't there? I don't think even Jared knows what he's thinking unless Marco wants him to know." She laid a hand on Sophie's shoulder. "I've never heard him talk about another woman, you know. I've seen him with a few, and it was painfully apparent that for him they were only casual dates. Now that I've met you, I understand why. He had you tucked away here at home waiting for him."

"It wasn't quite like that—"

"Still, I can tell by the way he acts that he cares for you a great deal. Jared said last night that he felt much better after meeting you."

"He's worried about Marco?"

"'Worried' is an understatement." Merry hesitated. "Did Marco tell you about his accident?"

Sophie smiled wryly, but there was no humor in it. "I managed to drag a few sentences out of him. I know he spent the night alone and injured in the jungle, and that the other people in the plane died. But as for how he's doing…he had a doctor's appointment yesterday, and all he would tell me—again—is that he's fine."

Merry shook her head sympathetically. "I'm not surprised. He won't discuss it even with Jared. Jared's the one who found him. Did you know?"

A jolt of shock, mingled with horrified surprise, shot through Sophie. "No. He's never said much about what happened."

"As soon as Jared heard about Marco's plane going down, he joined a search effort. His team found the plane. Of the three people who'd been in it, only Marco was still alive. His leg must have been really bad—Jared stayed with him in South America for almost a month. He says the doctors down there would have amputated if he hadn't been standing over them."

Sophie could imagine no doctor in his right mind would want to argue with Jared Adamson. The condensed version of the story gave her chills; what must it have been like for Marco? Quietly she said, "He really hates the limits he has to live with now, although he pretends it doesn't bother him. I wish he could let himself get angry, but he won't."

And it was true. She realized that in all the years she'd known Marco, she'd rarely, if ever, seen him lose control.

The cleanup took only a few moments more, and then Merry and she rejoined the men. To her surprise, Marco had given Jared his car keys and directions back to his condo. In the morning Jared and Merry would come by and pick up Marco for the return trip to the airport.

She was very aware of his dark presence at her side as they said good-night to his friends, and she hoped her discomfort didn't show. It was silly, she supposed, in this day and age, to be embarrassed about sleeping or living with a man to whom she wasn't married, and yet that's exactly how she felt.

When the door closed behind the Adamsons, she took a few steps into the living room, then turned and put her hands on her hips. "Your friends are very nice people. Thank you for introducing them to me. But in the future, I'd prefer that you be more discreet about our sleeping arrangements."

One black eyebrow rose. "Why?"

She glared at him for a long moment before she realized he was totally serious. "Marco...I don't like having people knowing that we're sleeping together. I mean, it's one thing for people to draw assumptions, but you practically painted a sign for your friends tonight."

He was studying her like she was one of the landforms he found so fascinating. "Your ideas are about a century behind the times," he informed her. "Jared and Merry don't care that we're living together."

"We're not living together," she said. "I live here. You live somewhere else."

"Not for long, though," he pointed out. "Why don't we set a wedding date tonight so that we can tell Jared and Merry in the morning? Maybe they could arrange to come in for the ceremony."

She stared at him. "Do you ever listen to a word I say?"

His face was losing its glow of good humor. "On occasion. I just screen the words when you aren't making any sense."

"Marco," she said, letting her exasperation color her tone, "I really did not appreciate you broadcasting the fact that you sleep here. Does that make sense to you?"

"Not really," he said. "Besides, I didn't appreciate the fact that you horned in and invited my friends to your apartment for dinner, so we're even."

Her mouth fell open. "What?" Then she rallied. "It's my apartment. I didn't need your permission."

"Well, it might have been nice to be consulted," he said, and the rising anger in his voice shocked her. "Do you think I enjoyed sitting here talking about old times? How much fun do you think it is for me to be reminded that there are things I can never do again?" His voice had risen to a roar. "Dammit, Sophie, I expected you to understand that!"

She was speechless. She was the one who'd been angry, and suddenly he was yelling at her! Her voice was a low, fierce whisper when she finally spoke. "How could I understand when you won't talk to me about how you feel?"

The low words hung in the charged atmosphere between them. Marco's eyes were angry, his jaw set. And though she normally wasn't given to displays of temper, she felt her own irritation flaring out of control.

"You've been hiding your feelings from me, from your family, even from your best friends, since you woke up in a South American hospital and realized your life had changed. Why didn't you let your parents know when you were hurt? Can you imagine how your mother must have felt, learning that one of her children had been lying alone in a hospital somewhere for more than a month? And then you wouldn't let them come when you were in rehab—my mother says they were frantic.'' She took a deep breath, caught her runaway tongue and attempted to gentle her tone. ''Marco, you can't think for other people. You can't control everything in the world.''

''I don't—''

''In fact—'' and the bitterness she carried deep inside seeped to the surface and spilled over ''—if you weren't so determined to be the one in control all the time, you and I could have been married for years by now!''

There was a shocked silence between them. Sophie put one hand to her mouth, unable to believe she'd spoken those words aloud.

Marco's tanned features darkened even more. ''That's what really gets to you, isn't it? I wouldn't let you tie me down—''

''I never wanted to tie you down,'' she shouted. Tears filled her eyes, even though she understood that he was lashing out, defending himself by taking the offensive. ''That's the most unfair statement I've ever heard. I would have waited here for you. I'd have gone with you to the jungle, I'd have lived in a one-room hut if you'd asked me.'' The tears overflowed and cascaded down her cheeks. ''But you never asked me, Marco. You made the decision without ever consulting me.''

''I wanted you with me.'' There was still anger in his tone, but now there was a weariness that disarmed her ire and urged her to offer him the comfort of her embrace. ''You'll never know how much I wanted to take you with me. And I'll admit it, I made a mistake.''

He crossed to her and wrapped her in his arms, using the tail of his shirt to blot her tears. ''I made a mistake,'' he repeated. ''And if you think I won't regret it for the rest of my life, then you can think again. Please,'' he said, his forehead pressed to hers, ''I don't want to fight with you,

Sophie. I'm sorry I got mad. It was just a tough evening. I had no right to take it out on you.''

"It's not a bad thing to let yourself get angry once in a while," she said. "It might even be good for you."

He smiled, but his eyes were shuttered, and once again he was a man alone. A man who gave her no clue as to what he was thinking. "There's no point in getting angry," he said, and there was a hopeless note in his voice that broke her heart. "There's nothing I can do to change the present or the past."

"But—"

He dropped his head and nuzzled his face into her neck, and his warm breath gusting over her flesh made her shiver. "I want to look at the future," he said in a low, husky tone. He took her by the hips and pulled her toward him, until their bodies were aligned in the sweet fit she was beginning to know so well, and his lips pressed little kisses along the sensitive cords in her neck. "I want to look at our future," he said.

The words made her tremble as he lifted his head and set his mouth on hers. He urged her to the floor on the rug before her small fireplace and when he removed her clothing with fingers that trembled and covered her with his hard, hot body, she wrapped her legs around his hips and urged him on until they were both straining and shaking, until passion crashed over their heads and left them gasping for breath. And later, in her pretty bed in her pretty room, when he drew her into his arms and kissed her forehead, she realized with sleepy satisfaction that for the first time ever, Marco had lost his iron grip on control with her tonight.

For a few fleeting seconds she'd gotten a glimpse of the tightly contained rage that seethed beneath his placid surface, but then he had changed the subject and turned on the

charm. And because she loved him, because she could see
the demons that chased him, though she didn't know exactly what they were, she had let him avoid the past yet
again.

Nine

"**I** like your Sophie."

Jared and Marco waited at the gate in the airport where the Adamsons would board a plane out of Chicago. Merry had gone to find a ladies' room, taking Kitty with her for one last diaper change before the flight.

Marco grinned smugly. "I like my Sophie, too." And he wished she hadn't had to work today. It would have been nice to have her beside him as he said goodbye to his closest friends.

Jared cast him a measuring glance. "I gather you two have been an item for a long time."

Marco grimaced. "Not exactly. She married somebody else while I was globe-trotting."

His friend's eyebrows rose. "And ditched him when you came home?"

Marco shook his head. "He died."

"Ah. That explains it."

"Explains what?" He wasn't sure he liked the knowing tone in Jared's voice.

"The look in her eyes." Jared nodded. "I thought I caught a little trace of melancholy when she thought nobody was looking."

The comment rubbed him the wrong way. "Sophie isn't sad. I'd know it if she wasn't happy."

"Just an observation." Jared raised his hands in a gesture of surrender. " I have, on rare occasions, been known to be wrong."

Marco snorted, but he let that pass. "Sophie and I have known each other since we were kids. Not like that, you idiot," he added, seeing Jared's arched brow and knowing smile. But then he had to be truthful. "Well, sort of like that. But she was too young. I couldn't ask her to follow me all over the world."

Jared nodded, the smile growing even wider. "I recognize this argument," he said. "It ran around in my head, too, after I met Merry. And you see where it got me." But the satisfaction in his friend's hard features told Marco he wouldn't have it any other way.

"Well, it's a moot point, now," Marco said, and his good spirits drained away. "Since I won't be doing any more globe-trotting, we're going to settle down in wedded bliss and have a houseful of little Italian bambinos for our mothers to fight over."

The hazel eyes regarding him had sharpened, and Marco could see his friend's quick brain sorting through the conversation. "You sound like you're resigned to your execution rather than anticipating marriage."

Marco reached for a laugh but barely managed it. "You've been in the bush so long you've forgotten how to converse."

"Right." Jared shook his head, eyed Marco consideringly. "I know it isn't Sophie—she's wild about you. And a blind man could figure out you love the woman, even if he couldn't see the sappy look on your face when you're together. So what's the deal?"

"There is no 'deal.'"

Jared didn't look convinced, but he was saved from answering anything more by the return of Merry and little Kitty, who threw herself at her father's knees, giggling and reaching up to be lifted. But as Jared swung his daughter up into his arms, his eyes met Marco's, and Marco was the first to look away.

Even a blind man could figure out you love the woman. As he took the steps to her condo that evening, Jared's words rang in his ears.

Maybe it was true, but he wasn't blind, and it had gotten past him. He needed her; he'd finally admitted that much, and he wanted her body. He liked her mind, respected her work and enjoyed the companionship they shared. But now the words had been said, and he couldn't make them go away.

He loved her. Hell, he'd loved her for a long, long time. He'd just been too stupid and stubborn to admit it. He'd taken the love she offered, and hadn't bothered to give his in return. It was a wonder she hadn't killed him by now. What was really a wonder was that she hadn't thrown him out when he turned up in her life again.

And then he remembered she nearly had. Sophie hadn't wanted to care for him, and the first time he'd shown up at her place it had been painfully obvious.

It gave him a warm, satisfied feeling to know that she'd been unable to resist him. And it made him feel strangely humble.

It was time to let her know he returned her love. It was

all she needed, he was sure, to make her happiness complete, to melt the small wall of reserve he sometimes sensed in her. She was uncertain of him, and because she was, she wasn't happy. That must have been what Jared had seen.

Well, he would change all that when he told her he loved her. He wanted to make Sophie happy.

And if a little part of him still grieved for the loss of the life he'd had, no one but him would ever know it. He had a new life now, and it would be enough. It would have to be.

She heard him the moment he came in and she started, looking down at the photos she'd been going through. Her pulse sped up and she felt the funny flutter in the pit of her stomach that she got whenever Marco was around. "I'm back here," she called. Quickly she replaced the lid on the box of photos she held, then set the box on a nearby desk with several others.

His footsteps sounded sure and heavy as he strode down the hall, and then he was there, framed in the doorway. Somehow he always seemed bigger in person than he was in her mind, and she noted the way his broad shoulders filled the entrance to the room.

"Hi." He stepped forward as she stood. And then he reached for her.

He hauled her into his arms as if he hadn't seen her in months, seeking her lips almost frantically and thrusting his tongue into her mouth, kissing her wildly, rubbing his palms up and down her back and pressing her firmly against his hard body.

His urgency communicated itself to her, and within seconds she was on fire, burning with need for him. When he began to open the top buttons of her blouse, she started from the bottom and met him halfway, and when he flicked open the front closure of her bra and immediately cupped his warm palms over the heavy weight of her breasts, she couldn't prevent the moan that escaped.

He looked down at her and his black eyes blazed with a primal demand.

Turning her back to him, he pushed her forward to rest over the desk that had been behind her, crowding into the spread vee of her legs until she could feel the whole hard length of him pressed against the soft crease of her bottom. He didn't even bother removing her panties, just pulled them aside and guided himself to the threshold of her yielding female portal, then thrust forward in one sure, swift move. The movement knocked a box of photos off the desk to scatter across the floor, but she barely noticed it.

It was an exquisite moment of overwhelming pleasure for her, invaded, impaled, held hostage to his need. The room was filled with the sound of harsh gasping breath and the flat slap of damp flesh driving against damp flesh; the hot male scent of him surrounded her. She could feel it beginning, a faraway demand that came closer and closer, faster and faster, tighter and tighter, until her abdomen drew into a clenched ball of need and suddenly exploded into heaving undulations as waves of satiation crashed within her.

Behind her, all movement stopped as his body went rigid and his hips arched deeply into her; she could feel the rhythmic pulsing of his own finish surging against the inner walls of her body and hear the low groans forced from his throat as he emptied himself into her. Then his muscles melted, and his weight slumped over her, carrying them both down onto the desk. His head lay beside hers; his face turned into the curve of her shoulder as he fought for breath.

Finally, he raised his weight from her. "Are you all right?" he whispered into her ear.

"No," she said, exhaling deeply.

"What's wrong?"

Sophie took a deep breath but before she could move, he slipped from her.

"I'm sorry," he said, standing behind her. "Sometimes I just need you so much that by the time I get home to you—"

"I'm fantastic," she interrupted.

"What?"

"I'm fantastic," she repeated. "Absolutely, positively wonderful. Don't apologize."

She felt his hand on her shoulder and as she straightened, he swung her into his arms and limped through the doorway and down the hall to her bedroom.

When he reached her bed, he set her on her feet long enough to tear back the covers before getting in and drawing her after him. And for a time she dozed, content, in his arms. *He needed her.*

Later she realized with a jolt of amusement that they hadn't even spoken beyond those few words they'd exchanged. "Was the Adamsons' flight on time this morning?" Idly she traced the heavy line of jet-black curls that bisected his chest, wandering out to brush her fingertip over one dark nipple until it puckered and stood out from the surrounding flesh.

"No problems," he reported. "After they left, I drove to Purdue and worked for the rest of the day."

"They're so lucky."

"Why? You mean the adorable munchkin? Yeah, she is something special, isn't she?" The warm affection in his voice scraped over the sore spot that her own childless state had left within her. Every time he talked of children, his voice softened and took on a caressing quality. He would make a wonderful father.

"Kitty is sweet, but that isn't what I meant." She sighed. "I envy them their freedom. It would be so exciting to be able to go to new places, meet new people, live in different climates and learn different customs."

"It's not all that fantastic," he said.

"Hah. They're going to Hawaii. Hawaii! To a girl who can count on one hand the times she's been more than a state away from home, that's exciting."

"You'd hate that life-style if you had no choice." Marco's voice had dropped flat and low. "You'd miss your family so much you'd do anything to get home."

Abruptly she realized why he felt so defensive. This had been his rationale for leaving her. So she continued stroking her finger over his torso, refusing to let him tell her how she felt. "It suited you. Why should I be any different?"

"Because."

"Ah. I see."

"You don't see anything," he informed her. He rolled to his side, facing her, and slid one big palm across the soft flesh of her belly. "You don't realize what a support network your family is. And there's a real comfort in living in a familiar environment."

"So why didn't you?"

That stopped him cold. He was quiet for a minute. Then he lifted himself on one elbow, leaning over her. "You talk too much sometimes," he informed her.

She smiled sweetly. "Changing the subject?"

"Umm-hmm." The hand that lay over her slipped lower, and she caught her breath as one long finger feathered over the sensitive skin on the inside of her thighs. He moved the finger higher and she caught her breath as her body began to hum. "I like this subject a lot better," he informed her.

And as she wound her arms around his neck and pulled his head down to hers, she confessed, "So do I."

Another hour passed, and when Marco's stomach rumbled, she laughed. "Oops. Guess we forgot one of the body's basic needs."

"Yeah, but we satisfied the most important one." Marco grinned as he rose from the bed and pulled on his pants.

She rose, too, and drew on one of his T-shirts. It was so large it reached halfway to her knees. She started to retrieve her panties, but Marco kicked them beyond her reach and took her by the hand.

"Hey!" she protested. "I need those."

"No, you don't." His grin was enough to halt her heartbeat all over again and she shook her head in wonder. "Don't you ever think of anything else?"

He laughed. "Yeah—when you're not around." He slung an arm over her shoulders, and she put hers around his waist as they started down the hall. It was a warm, casual intimacy that felt so right it nearly brought tears to her eyes.

But Marco didn't notice. He pulled her to a halt at the door to the spare bedroom. "What a mess. Wonder why I didn't see this before?"

She laughed, recalling the wild lovemaking that had sent the boxes crashing to the floor.

But when he started forward, she tugged at his hand. "Leave it. I can clean it up later. Let me get you something to eat."

It was too late. He already had bent over and retrieved the box, then started scooping up photos from the stack spilled across the floor. His movements slowed as he flipped through photo after photo. He was seeing himself, she knew, because only hours before she'd been looking through those very same pictures, images of his life from high school and on throughout the years. After they'd begun to date, there were many, many more. Any time they'd spent time together, she'd taken her camera along. When he went away again, those photos had been all she had left.

Finally, he raised his head. "You kept all these pictures?" He looked stunned.

She nodded, uncomfortably aware that the act spoke volumes about the depths of her feelings for him. She'd never been able to bring herself to toss them out, though she'd always been careful that Kirk didn't see them; he didn't deserve to be hurt like that.

"Why?" His tone was quiet, as if he were genuinely bewildered.

She shrugged. "It helped me to keep you close when I hadn't seen you in a long time." She took the box from his hands and straightened the photos enough to close the lid. But as she turned to set it back on the desk, Marco closed the space between them and drew her back against his body.

"I didn't need pictures," he said, wrapping his arms around her from behind. "Any time I liked, I could picture your face in my head." He made a sound that was halfway between annoyed and amused. "Half the time, you were there even when I didn't want to be thinking about you. Do you know I once had a woman throw a crystal vase at me after I called her Sophie during—" He suddenly seemed to recognize the dubious wisdom of completing his sentence. "Well, anyway, she wasn't very happy."

"Too bad for you." She couldn't keep the fierce satisfaction from her voice as she slipped out of his arms. "I hope she had good aim." The hurt that had sprung at her, all the more vicious for having been unsuspected, drew her body into taut, tense lines. She'd known there had to be other women through the years; Merry Adamson had even mentioned them. But they hadn't been real until now, and she found she couldn't bear reality.

"Sophie, I—"

She turned and raised a hand, palm out, pushing his explanations away. "Don't. Just don't. You made it clear that we had no strings between us. We were both free agents." Furious at him for spoiling what had been a special evening, and equally furious with herself for reacting, she headed for the doorway. "I'm going to reheat something for dinner."

She busied herself setting two places at her little glass table with its ice-cream-parlor-style chairs in the kitchen nook and making a small meal.

A few minutes later he joined her in the kitchen. He didn't mention their last exchange and neither did she. They spoke little during dinner. When they did, they both were stilted and polite, and she was grateful that it was short. He helped her clear the table and put away the dishes, and it struck her that he always helped in the kitchen, that he never expected her to wait on him. In fact, often the reverse was true. He was a credible cook and sometimes had dinner waiting for her when he beat her home in the evening.

She glanced at him as he reached to store wineglasses on a high shelf, and she thought that even with a dish towel slung over his shoulder, he was one of the most masculine men she knew. He'd put on a pair of khaki shorts, and the muscles in his legs shifted and bunched as he moved. The scarred right knee was so much a part of him she didn't even notice it anymore.

Without warning, tears stung behind her eyes and she turned away. She might want to strangle him right now, but oh, how she loved him. He'd owned her heart her whole life long. How could she bear to give him up?

But the answer was clear. She had no choice.

He would go away again one day, no matter how badly she wished it could be otherwise. And when he did, she would smile and say goodbye if it killed her, because she had gone into this with her eyes wide-open; she knew what to expect.

This talk of marriage would fade as his leg healed more and he realized he didn't have to stay here. She refused to believe there were no possibilities for fieldwork for him out there.

He let her avoid him, hold him at arm's length, until the lights were out and they were both settled in her bed for the night. But there was no way he was going to let her brush the fight—if that's what it had been—aside and ignore him.

Reaching out, he snagged her hand. The feel of her small fingers linked with his eased the constriction around his heart a little, and he simply lay there holding her hand for a while. He hadn't meant to hurt her earlier. Each of them had moved ahead without the other in the years he'd been away, and he guessed it was time he faced it.

"What was your husband like?"

Her whole body tensed. "Thoughtful. Kind. Gentle. Why?"

"Just wondered." He shrugged. "And you said you were married for about a year?"

"Sixteen months, one week and two days." Her voice had dropped to a low monotone.

The precise way she recounted the time shook him a little. She hadn't given any indication that she was thinking so much about any other man, even her husband. He didn't like it, though he knew he was a jerk for resenting a dead man, when he, Marco, had chosen to let her go free to marry that man.

But all he said was, "And you told me he was a farmer."

"He was going to farm," she corrected. "He worked here in Chicago for a little while after we were married."

"You loved him?"

She sat up and twisted to look down at him as if she wasn't sure she had heard him right, her eyes wide with shock. Then she sprang off the bed so fast he didn't have time to grab for her.

"What are you asking?" Her voice was suddenly aggressive, more so than he'd ever heard her, and her finely arched brows were a study in fury. "Exactly what do you want to know, Marco? Was he my only other lover? Was he a good lover? Did I love him?" She paused and took a deep breath, holding up a finger in warning when he would have spoken. "All right. Here are your answers. Yes, he was my only lover, other than you. I cried the first time, and he was upset. He thought he'd hurt me. But the reason I was crying was because he wasn't you, because I'd always imagined that you would be the only man who—"

"Sophie—"

But she didn't stop. "Yes, he was a good lover. Good enough for me, even if it didn't come close to being like it is with you." Tears had formed in the corners of her eyes. As she gestured wildly, one overflowed its boundary and streamed down her cheek, followed by a second, and then another and another. "And did I love him? Yes, in a way. But I never loved Kirk the way I love you."

He reached for her then, but she slapped his hands away. "Does that make you happy? Knowing that there were three people in my marriage, and one of them was you?" She began to sob aloud. "Do you have any idea how guilty that makes me feel? That I married a wonderful, adoring man that *I didn't love,* that my sweet husband died without ever knowing he wasn't the one who held my heart?"

He reached for her again, pulling her to him despite her struggles to push him away, and as she began to sob in earnest, he simply rocked her and let her cry. When she began to calm a little, he drew her to the bed and sat down on the edge of the mattress with her in his lap.

"Down deep, I expected to come home and find you waiting for me." It was a hard confession to make; he had to force himself to utter the words. For so long, he'd told himself that he didn't need Sophie to make his life complete.... "It was selfish, and stupid, and wrong, and I have no right to be jealous. But I am."

She sighed, and it was a sad, dead sound that tore at his heart. "If you knew how many nights I lay there wishing the arms around me were yours...."

He hadn't cried in years. Even when he lay in a hospital bed praying that he wouldn't lose his leg, he hadn't cried. But now he had to swallow the lump that rose as he cradled Sophie in his arms and pressed a kiss to her temple. "I'm so sorry, sweetheart."

"Kirk asked me to marry him on Valentine's Day the year after our college graduation. I didn't know what to say. We'd been friends since our freshman year, and we'd dated occasionally. After graduation we dated more steadily." She took a deep breath, then lifted her head and looked him in the eye. "But I was still waiting for you. I hadn't heard a word from you since—since the time we made love, but I still was convinced you'd come back for me." She shook her head at her own stupidity.

How many men were lucky enough to find a woman like this? If he'd been in her shoes, he wasn't sure he could forgive so readily. Why did she still love him?

She plowed on, seemingly determined to get the story out now that she'd started. "When Kirk proposed, I wasn't really surprised. He'd been hinting at it for a while, but I had never committed myself. But then, when it became real, it was as if someone threw a bucket of cold water in my face. I realized that I was wasting my life waiting for a man who probably hadn't given me a second thought since we'd said goodbye, that this might be the best chance I had for happiness.''

"I did think of you,'' he said in a low voice. "Nothing I can say will change the past, but you were always the one I thought of when I imagined myself settling down.''

"But I didn't know that,'' she pointed out. "So after a week of mourning, of saying goodbye to my dreams, I said yes to Kirk. We got married in May.'' She slid off Marco's lap and walked across the room to her dresser, idly fingering the silver-backed comb and mirror that lay there. She turned to face him, and her eyes were so bleak and despairing it frightened him. "One day I came home and Kirk was sitting in the kitchen. I knew right away something terrible had happened. We'd been friends for six years—he couldn't hide anything from me.''

Her breath hitched, and Marco put out a hand. After a moment's hesitation, she came across the room and took his hand, seating herself beside him on the bed. He laced his fingers tightly through hers, wishing he could erase the horror she'd been through from her mind and replace it with only good memories, memories that included him. How had he gone through his life without realizing he couldn't live without Sophie? How could he have been so blind for so long?

But she didn't hear the agonizing questions pounding through his head, and she continued speaking, telling him her story, a story about which he wanted desperately to know every detail, and yet he could barely stand to hear her soft voice.

"Not long after the wedding Kirk had been having some

back pain. I thought it went away, but it was getting worse. He didn't tell me because he didn't want to worry me. He finally went to a doctor when the pain was so bad he couldn't take it. He expected the doctor to tell him he had a disk problem, or that he should start seeing a chiropractor...but he was diagnosed with pancreatic cancer. It had already metastasized—he had a huge abdominal lump that was causing the back pain, but it had spread to other places as well."

Now her voice sounded calm and matter-of-fact, and he realized she'd told this part of the story many times before.

"He started treatment, but they didn't give us much false hope," she said. "A few years, if we were lucky. The next autumn, he got the flu at the beginning of October and he never completely recovered. Three weeks later, he died."

Her words echoed around the silent room for a moment, then they, too, faded away until the air was thick with the absence of sound.

Marco cleared his throat. He didn't know exactly what to say; he wanted to take away her pain, and the worst thing in the world was the realization that he was helpless. That part of her life was forever lost to him, emotions and memories he could never share—

"Until recently, I wished I had died, too."

The image that rose with her words was shocking. He squeezed her fingers gently, his mind spinning with the notion of a world without Sophie in it. "I'm glad you didn't," he said quietly. "I'm sorry Kirk died." He wondered if she realized that was the first time he'd ever spoken her husband's name.

Other than the first time they'd made love again, he'd avoided thinking about the other man. It was simply easier to pretend he'd never existed. But that was no longer an option. Sophie had trusted him with her deepest hurts, her darkest memories, and they forever would be his, as well.

She stood then, catching him off guard, and before he could speak she had climbed into his lap, straddling him with her legs and winding her arms around his neck. "Love me," she whispered. "I need you."

He wrapped both arms around her, pulling her close and pressing her soft body against all the hard angles of his. The feel of her soft flesh pressed against him elicited a response he'd have sworn he couldn't give again for a few hours, but he kept his mouth gentle and tender as he took hers. He wanted to tell her how much he loved her, that he needed her, too, but he sensed she needed time to simply feel, to reassure herself that she was alive, that he was alive, that what they had between them was real.

Tomorrow, he promised himself before the heat they generated burned out all conscious thought. *I'll tell her tomorrow.*

Ten

Marco was taking her out to dinner.

Sophie stood on the stoop in front of his condo and checked her watch. He'd asked her to meet him at his place at six, but she was a few minutes early and it looked as though she'd beaten him here.

Digging out the key he'd given her when he took possession, she let herself in and dropped her purse in the nearest chair.

Make that the only chair. He'd done very little to furnish his place. A masculine leather couch and chair with two brass-and-glass tables and a single floor lamp completed the living room. In the kitchen he'd done even less, dispensing with a table altogether in favor of two stools at the bar dividing the kitchen from the living area.

Though he'd never said so, she knew why he wasn't expending a lot of time or energy on this condo. He didn't expect to be here very long. He was doing everything in his power to get her to agree to marry him quickly.

The familiar ache settled around her heart.

But over the past weeks, as he'd cajoled, teased, persuaded and argued in favor of marriage, she'd caught herself dreaming that this could last. He'd been so caring and protective, so determined not to let her shut him out of her life, that she was beginning to hope that maybe he did care deeply for her. He hadn't said so, yet, but she knew those words wouldn't come easily to him. He'd been independent for a long time, and she knew Marco well enough to know that he never did anything without thinking it through from every angle first.

Was it too much to hope for? Her heart didn't think so, no matter how she cautioned herself.

He'd been so wonderful last night, so gentle and tender. She still felt wrung out, slightly raw around the edges, from the emotional toll that speaking of her life with Kirk had exacted. Only Marco's soothing attentions had eased the hurt that had risen again to torment her. Even so, all day, she'd operated in a fog, gone through her caseload at work on automatic pilot.

When he had called and asked her if she wanted to go out to dinner, her first impulse was to decline, to suggest they stay in and have a quiet evening. But she didn't have the energy to cook, and she figured he probably didn't, either, if he was suggesting they eat out.

She walked down the hall to the bathroom and washed her face and hands, then brushed her hair. Ah, better. She'd come straight from work and she felt slightly grubby, but Marco had specified six and she hadn't had time to go home.

As she walked back down the hall, she noticed the door of his extra bedroom ajar. He used it as an office, she knew, and he'd just purchased a gleaming mahogany desk at an auction a week ago. Stepping into the room, she checked out the look of the piece of furniture.

But before she could really see it, her attention was caught by the pieces of paper spread all over the room. No, not spread, she thought, thrown. The floor was littered with papers, scattered helter-skelter as if an impatient hand had swept them from a neat pile, some twisted and crumpled, others torn completely in half.

What on earth…? Kneeling, she automatically began to gather up some of the mess, glancing at the papers that weren't too badly damaged to read, wondering if anything important had found its way into the trash heap. She smiled fondly. Marco had been so neat and tidy at her place; she never would have suspected that he was such a slob.

But her smile faded as she read the words. Puzzlement replaced it.

"Name: Marco C. Esposito, Ph.D.…Stanford University…applicants must complete all parts of the attached form…."

She looked at another, and then another.

"Seismic exploration…Universidad de Buenos Aires…geological surveying expedition of Egypt… Royal Melbourne Institute of Technology…three-month commitment to reconstruct and interpret lake histories…expedition funded in part by the University of Edinburgh….

What on earth…?

And then she knew. She had trouble taking the next deep breath. A fifty-pound weight settled directly on her chest, forcing her to take shallow, careful pants as she slowly turned her head and surveyed the chaos around her.

She was sitting in the middle of Marco's dreams...
dreams that didn't include her.

Dozens upon dozens of applications for expeditions, for
fieldwork opportunities, for geological exploration that
would take him far from her and from home, were filled
out. Each blank was meticulously filled with neat typing or
Marco's distinctive block printing, from a listing of his ed-
ucational background to his previous expedition experiences. But when the listings of physical requirements began, the blanks were conspicuously empty. Many of the
viciously ripped sheets of paper were torn directly across
the section dealing with physical capabilities.

Numbed disbelief gave way to a hurt so wide and deep
she wanted to throw herself into the chasm and howl out
her pain. All the time Marco had been romancing her—this
time, as all the others—he'd been dreaming of getting away
from Chicago and back to doing what he loved best.

What he loved far more than he could ever care for her.

The truth was a sharp blade cleaving through all her silly
imaginings, neatly slicing away any hope she had of making a life with Marco. All the time she'd been so touched
by his concentrated attentions, she'd been nothing more
than a means of keeping Marco from fretting about the
restrictions his knee injury imposed on the life-style he
loved. His second choice.

The wreckage around her was evidence of the pain that
tormented him, pain he'd hidden from her, refusing to let
her share in the feelings he was experiencing as if she were
no more important than any casual relationship. And she
supposed that she wasn't. He never got angry. Several times
she'd watched him gather his control and slide rage back
into a compartment of his mind, covering it with charm,
with flippant banter. Shutting her out so that he could go
his own way as he had all his life.

She was terribly cold, though the air-conditioning wasn't set high, and she wrapped her arms protectively around herself, rocking forward, huddling in the middle of the wreckage of her life. She was too shattered to realize tears were called for, so she merely sat, wilted and waiting for the nurturing she realized she now knew she would never receive.

Marco opened the door with a smile on his face and one hand behind his back. Sophie loved Chicago's special Fannie May chocolates. And she would love this box more than usual. He'd had a ring designed for her, and finally it was ready, so he'd spent the day racing around making preparations for a memorable evening. The ring was hidden inside the box; he carried a bag with candles and champagne, as well as a fresh bouquet he'd just picked up from the florist. Tonight the waiting would end. Tonight he planned to formally propose, to tell her he loved her, to end the dodging and evasions he'd allowed and get Sophie to set a wedding date.

She wasn't in the living room, and he frowned, seeing that she wasn't in the kitchen, either.

Setting down the candy box, the bag and the flowers, he walked down the hall. Maybe she'd decided to rest on his bed while she waited. She'd looked tired and drained this morning, and he'd worried about her all day.

As he passed the door of his office, something distracted him from his search. He took three more steps toward the bedroom before his feet slowed. He pivoted, a feeling of dread congealing in his gut. He normally kept that door closed.

As he reached the door of his office—the open door—the feeling of dread increased.

Sophie sat on the floor in front of his desk, the trash can beside her.

"What are you doing in here?" He knew his voice was sharp; he was struggling for calm.

She didn't answer him, and his uneasiness metamorphosed into anger. "This door was closed for a reason. Why are you snooping around in here?"

Her head came up then, and her eyes met his. He couldn't read anything in her expression, but the dull, glazed look in her eyes sent alarm surging through him. "I'm sorry," she said in a polite, distant little voice. "The door was open. I was going to clean up...."

She made a vague movement with her hand, then shook her head as if she forgot what she was going to say. With the creaky movements of a person many times her age, she carefully lifted herself from the floor and came toward the door. As she rose, scraps of paper fluttered away from her skirt.

"Sophie?" Marco didn't budge from his place in the doorway. So she'd seen the applications he'd filled out and then shredded during the first days he'd been here. Why was she acting like this?

"I'm going home," she said in a weary tone, stopping well short of him. "Please let me pass."

"Not until you tell me what you're thinking." He folded his arms, gripping the opposite biceps with his big hands until his fingers dug into muscle. Inside, panic was writhing and seething, boiling ever closer to the iron control he imposed on himself.

She closed her eyes for a moment, and when she opened them, there was a shadowed knowledge, a deep painful hopelessness that he'd never seen before. "I'm thinking I've been a fool," she said. "Again."

"Why?"

"Because I should have learned my lesson the last time you left."

"I'm not going anywhere."

"But I am," she said. She took a deep breath, and her voice was stronger when she spoke again. "I deserve more than to be used for a distraction to keep your mind off the fact that you can't travel anymore."

"You can't leave!" he roared, and the desperation in his gut colored his voice. The control he so carefully wore vanished as his anxiety increased. "I'm not using you. What we have is important to me. Don't you understand? My life, the life I had, is over. I can't ever leave again. I'm going to be stuck behind a desk for the rest of my working days."

"And you've been using me to forget that."

"That's not true!"

"No?" She gestured at the wreckage of the room around them. "Then what's this? Can you look me in the eye and tell me that you would have come back here, back to me, if you hadn't torn up your knee?"

Silence fell between them for one second, then two and three and four. And he saw what little light remained in her eyes dim and die. He couldn't lie. Until he'd come home again he had never let himself acknowledge how badly he'd needed her. "It doesn't matter why I came back," he insisted, trying to erase the moment when he'd hesitated. "I'm here and I'm staying and we're getting married and starting a family."

But she was shaking her head. For the first time he saw a sheen of tears in her eyes but she kept speaking. "No, Marco, we aren't."

"You have to," he insisted, completely thrown by her implacable certainty. He couldn't lose her! "You're the only woman I've ever wanted to be the mother of my children."

Sophie visibly shrank in on herself, drawing into a small, stiff block of a body that practically shouted, "No touching allowed." He wanted to reach for her, but he could sense that the thin thread with which she was hanging on to her composure was stretched to the breaking point.

"You're not the settling down kind, Marco," she said quietly. "And we'd both be lying to ourselves if we pretend you are." She bowed her head then, and he could see that she had become a smooth, blank wall off which any words would bounce; there was no point in trying to talk to her now.

Slowly he stepped aside, and she practically bolted through the doorway. In an instant he heard the front door slam, and he stood unmoving while her engine started up and she drove away.

She was wrong! He'd known she had reservations, but all the while—all this time—she'd been expecting him to leave her again. She hadn't trusted him to stay, to care for her. Still, in the past few weeks she'd begun to let down her guard. He'd known she was releasing her determination to resist him, and he'd reveled in it.

It was only now that he realized how precious a gift she had given him. He'd hurt her deeply when he'd walked away from her before. A second chance was a lot to ask, and he hadn't asked, he'd demanded.

He'd taken, taken, taken from Sophie and had given her so little in return. He hadn't even told her he loved her, he suddenly remembered.

And if he tried to tell her now, she'd never believe him.

As he stood in the doorway, looking at the ruined applications, it came to him again that the life he wanted wasn't off somewhere around the globe. It had been right here in Chicago all the time, and he'd been too stupid to see it until it was too late.

He alternately paced and forced himself to sit, killing the rest of the lonely evening. Sophie had been so distraught that he knew she needed time; it would do neither of them any good if he showed up at her place tonight.

He slept badly and very little, and when the clock told him it was morning, he rushed through showering and getting dressed, forgetting breakfast altogether. If he hurried, he could catch Sophie before she went to work. He couldn't wait one more minute to get things settled between them.

As he drove to her condo, confidence began to grow within him again. He'd tell her he loved her. She'd listen when he explained that those applications had been filled out weeks ago, right after he'd first come home. Before he'd realized that everything he wanted was right here. He wasn't waiting a day longer to start living the rest of his life with the woman he loved.

She wasn't home.

He was disappointed, deeply so, but not panicked. He'd known her to go in to work early on occasion. If she'd slept as badly as he, she probably decided she might as well go do something useful since she couldn't sleep, he thought, driving the expressway toward downtown. Well, she had a surprise coming.

She wasn't at work.

"I'm sorry," said a pleasant-faced woman whose name tag read "Josephina" behind the secretary's desk. "Sophie is going to be out of the office for a few weeks. May I give her a message?"

No, dammit, Josephina could not give her a message.

As he climbed into his car and drove back to the northwestern suburbs, his mind was whirling with confusion and a meltdown of the calm he'd imposed on himself in the secretary's office. Where could she have gone?

She couldn't just take off without telling him.

Of course she could. *As far as she knows, there's nothing holding her to you. Did you give her any reason to think there was?*

Yes. Yes, he had. Maybe not in so many words, but surely she knew how he felt about her.

Didn't she?

Her mother hadn't heard from her. Neither had any other members of her family, and he had the added guilt of making them worry. He didn't know of any other place she might have gone, and there was nothing else to do but go home.

At eight that evening the telephone rang. He'd been hoping all day that she would call; he practically leaped over the bar to get to the phone. "Hello?"

But it wasn't Sophie. It was her sister Vee, and he listened numbly as she explained in halting, embarrassed phrases that they had heard from Sophie, that she had asked them to tell Marco she was fine and not to worry, that she had specifically requested that they not share her location with him.

He hung up in dazed silence. All his adult life he'd known Sophie was there, loving him, waiting for him. There'd never been a day when he'd doubted that, until he'd come home to learn she had married. And even then his doubt had been short-lived and his world had returned to normal the first time Sophie came into his arms.

Now there was no Sophie in his world, and nothing else mattered. Nothing at all.

Wisconsin was even more pleasant in the summer than it had been during the autumns she'd visited there. Her

cabin was tucked in among cool trees and she could walk
down to the lake for a swim anytime she liked.

She could have been in a jail cell for all the notice she
gave her surroundings.

Someday the pain would ease. She had to keep telling
herself that or she'd have been tempted to swim out to the
middle of the lake and let herself sink. But her life had
been crushed before, and she'd survived. And the pain had
gone away. Even though she wanted to scream and weep
every time she thought of Marco, even though she didn't
ever recall feeling quite so devastated or despairing when
Kirk died, she would survive this.

And if she repeated that often enough, maybe someday
she'd even believe it.

All she did, day and night, was think of him. A thousand
little things reminded her of him during the day. She would
see an unusual rock formation she knew he'd enjoy, she'd
want to share a loon's call, some phrase on the television
would remind her of something he'd said, a set of broad
shoulders would make her heart leap until she realized it
wasn't him.

He was in her dreams at night, sometimes tender and
pleading, sometimes angry and pushing her away. And always she woke with her pillow soaked by tears and her
eyes swollen and sore from the tears she'd shed in her
sleep.

Six weeks passed. July wore away and August came. She
called her family every Sunday. They were fine, they
missed her, they begged her to come home. And they all
carefully avoided any mention of Marco or anything re-
motely related to him.

One day in the middle of the month her telephone rang.
She lifted her head from the book she was reading and

stared at the phone, uncomprehending. Then she realized it was her phone and her job to answer it.

Who could be calling her first thing in the morning? She knew no one up here. She spoke to her family every weekend. They rarely called her, and they always called in the evening when they did. Anxiety rose. Had something happened to someone in her family?

She rushed across the room and snatched up the receiver. "Hello?"

"Hello, Sophie?" It was a tentative, troubled female voice she didn't recognize. "This is Dora Esposito."

"Mrs. E!" Marco's mother! What could she possibly be calling for? "How did you get this number?"

She hadn't meant the question to sound accusatory, but there was a hesitant silence at the other end of the line. "I, ah, copied it off your mama's telephone list," the older woman confessed.

"Oh." What should she say to that? "Is there something you needed? Is something wrong with Mama?" The last burst out of her in a rush of fear.

"No, no," Dora said hastily. "Your family's fine."

Did she imagine it, or had there been an emphasis on the word *your?* "That's good, then," she said. "And your family? Are they all well?" She wanted badly to ask about Marco but she forced back the words. Marco wasn't hers to ask after anymore.

"Sophie…I'm not the kind of mother who sticks her nose into her children's business…you know that, I hope."

"Of course." So she wanted to talk about Marco. Sharp knives of pain stabbed. She wondered when she'd be able to hear his name without wanting to cry. It occurred to her that if merely thinking of him was bad, actually seeing him again was going to destroy her.

"The thing is, Marco's not well."

"Not well?" Fear gripped her, strangling the words in her throat. "What's the matter with him?"

"He won't tell me," his mother said. "He won't eat. He doesn't look as if he's slept a wink since you left. I don't know what happened between you, dear, but I'll beg if it will change your mind. Please come home and talk to him. You're the only one he might talk to." There was a muffled sound that she thought was a sob, and Dora said, " I can't just sit and watch him die."

Late the same afternoon she pulled into the parking lot before Marco's condo, cut the engine and simply sat for a moment, willing the rising flood of feelings inside her back into some semblance of calm.

She'd panicked, totally and completely, at the thought that Marco might be dying. It wasn't until she was packed and halfway back to Elmwood Park that she realized that Mrs. Esposito probably hadn't meant it literally. But it wasn't a chance she was willing to take. She'd lost one man she cared for; she wasn't about to lose another. Even if he didn't want her anymore, wouldn't thank her for interfering, she had to try.

His car was in the parking lot, and she took several deep breaths, preparing herself for a face-to-face meeting. Approaching the front door, she rang his bell, but no one answered, though she leaned on it twice more and listened for footsteps. Nothing. Mrs. Esposito must have been exaggerating, then. If Marco was well enough to be out and about, he wasn't dying.

Fishing out the key she still carried, she inserted it into the lock and twisted the knob. The door swung inward.

Immediately she was struck by the darkness. The blinds at the windows were tightly closed. Her eyes, adjusted to the bright light outside, saw nothing but blackness for a moment, but gradually she began to make out shapes and textures, dim colors and shadowed corners.

And her eyebrows rose in shock.

The place was a mess. No, not a mess, a wreck. A complete and total wreck. Newspapers littered the floor, dropped where they'd been read, apparently. The lone recliner was askew, awkwardly sticking out into the middle of the room. Beside the door, not far from her feet, a black briefcase, stuffed to overflowing with ragged-edged papers, had been tossed against a closet door. Soda cans, beer cans and empty cups lay helter-skelter on the carpet around it, and an afghan which usually lay over the back of the couch, straggled across the carpet and reached vainly for the kitchen.

The kitchen. Pizza boxes, dirty dishes, milk cartons and empty cans. Everywhere. The dishwasher hung open, overflowing with crusted plates and glasses with liquids still congealed on their bottoms. A steady plinking drip from the faucet was the only sound in the whole place.

She took a tentative step forward, skirting around a paper plate with a half-eaten apple, brown and withered on it—

''What do you want?''

She gasped and her head jerked up as one hand flew to her throat. Marco stood in the hallway leading back to the bedroom. He wore nothing but a pair of ragged cutoff sweatpants, and even through the dusky light, she could see his jaw was dark with stubble.

He was the worst-looking thing she'd ever seen, and the best-looking, as well, and as they stared at each other through the gloom of his home, her heart swelled and burst wide-open with love. This was the man she wanted. Pride had no place here, nor did other people's conventional view of relationships.

There was nothing else, no one else in the world who

would ever make her feel like he could, and she'd take whatever crumbs he could give her in between excursions. It was almost the twenty-first century, but she was willing to keep the home fires burning for her man and wait as long as he asked her to wait.

Because without him, she was nothing.

Was she real? Or had he called up her image out of his desperate need for her?

Marco stared at Sophie's image, willing her to be real, to be here. She still hadn't responded to his question in any way, and he kicked newspapers and trash out of his way as he crossed to stand in front of her.

She wore slim-fitting bike shorts and an oversize T-shirt, her favorite low-key clothing for hanging out around the house. Curls bounced in a frothy tumble around her face from a whimsical ponytail gathered high on her head, and her huge sunglasses were stuffed carelessly in the side pocket of the handbag she had slung over her shoulder.

"You came back." It was a stupid thing to say, but he felt pretty stupid.

"I came back." Her voice was soft and sweet, her eyes a liquid pool of warmth. Did he dare hope that maybe she still cared for him? She reached up a hand and touched the side of his face, a fleeting brush of fingers that caused him to close his eyes against the need that raced through him. "You've lost weight," she said.

"I haven't felt much like eating." He cleared his throat. "Where did you go?"

A spasm of something that looked like pain twisted her face for an instant, and he saw her square her shoulders. "I went to a cabin by a lake in Wisconsin," she said. "I've been there before. It was a good place to get away and think."

He knew when she must have gone there first—after her husband died. Longing rose, with a tremendous desire to make her happy again. He wanted to take her in his arms and cuddle her, comfort her, cherish her. If she would let him.

But she was speaking again and he forced himself to listen. "Your mother called me," she said. "She's worried about you."

His heart sank. Had she come only because his mother had asked her to? "I didn't mean to worry anyone," he said, and it was true. He'd been so devastated when he'd realized Sophie was gone that he'd simply shut down, gone into human hibernation and forgotten the rest of the world and his responsibilities to it.

"You asked me why I was here." She looked up at him, and her eyes were dark and steady on his. "I came to tell you that I want to be with you. That without you I'm not really living. That I don't care if you only stay an hour or a day, that I'll always be waiting for you. You don't have to marry me. You can have me free." An expression of uncertainty crossed her face. "If you still want me."

Dear God. If he wanted her? She humbled him. She had loved him for so long and he had failed to value that love as he should have. It was a miracle that she still cared. Elation began to race along his nerve endings, and a building euphoria swelled within him. He was going to worship her every day for the rest of their lives, treasure her as he should have all along.

Slowly, gently, he reached out and took her hands in his, lacing his fingers through hers, and he saw her consciously relax at the link. He knew just how she felt.

"Oh, I still want you," he said. "I want you more than you'll ever know." He raised her hands to his lips and pressed a kiss to the back of each. "Is this how you felt when I left you?"

She blinked. "What?"

"Like there was no point in living. Like it didn't matter if the sun never rose again or the earth stopped turning. Is that how you felt when I went away and left you behind?"

She blinked again. And then her eyes filled with tears. "Yes," she whispered.

He could tell from her expression that she didn't fully understand. And it was important to him that she did. "I don't want you free," he said. "When you left, something inside me died. I love you. I want you back, but I want my ring on your finger and your promise that you'll never leave me again."

She smiled through a sniffle. "That sounds funny coming from *you*."

He grimaced. "I'll promise, too. I thought my life was over when I had the accident. I focused so completely on what I'd be losing from my life-style that I missed something far more important." He shrugged and shook his head. "I don't know why I couldn't let myself admit how important you are to me until I thought you had left. Sheer idiocy?"

Sophie shook her head, slipping her fingers from his and trailing them up over his arms and shoulders, up his neck and cheeks to tap lightly at his temples. "Not idiocy. Control. Loving means not being in control of everything that happens in your world. It means placing your trust in another person. You weren't ready for that." She smiled again, but the edges of it trembled and broke. "You don't have to pretend for me," she said. "I won't press you for anything you don't want to give."

She stopped, but only because he put one large palm over her mouth, cutting off her words. "Now who's being idiotic?'' The pain he'd given her stunned him; the depths of her doubt of his love and commitment shook him to the core, and he thanked God for this additional chance.

He looked deep into her eyes. ''Sophie, please come back to me. Marry me and stay with me until we're both old and gray and we've shared the kind of lives our parents have.''

Over his hand, her eyes were huge, shell-shocked. She was stone still.

Slowly he took his hand away and tugged her closer, holding her lightly by the hips. ''Say something,'' he said. ''You're making me nervous.''

''I—''

''I love you,'' he said again. ''I'll have to say it a lot to make up for keeping it hidden for so long. Will you please marry me?''

Slowly, her eyes still on his, she nodded. ''I'll marry you,'' she whispered. Her arms crept up around his neck. ''Oh, yes, I'll marry you!''

He exhaled heavily as he pulled her fully against him, loving the soft swell of female flesh that gave beneath his hands. ''Thank God.''

He put his hands beneath her bottom and lifted her into closer contact with his aching male flesh, groaning as she squirmed and wrapped her legs around his waist. He kissed her again, plunging his tongue deep and loving the unquestioning way she accepted him and returned his kisses.

But as he moved to carry her across the room, she tore her mouth away from his. ''Oh, no, you don't. There is no way you're laying me down on anything in this filthy place! The first thing we do tomorrow is clean.''

''All right.'' Chuckling, he stopped and pivoted, brought

her back to rest against the wall as he thrust strongly against her. "So who said anything about laying you down?"

She laughed, twining her arms around his neck and curling into his arms, and he breathed in her gentle scent in relief. Finally everything in his world was going to be right.

Epilogue

Three weeks later Sophie tossed her bridal veil over both their heads as they ducked birdseed thrown by the guests who had attended their wedding. Marco had her hand in his, and he raced for the limo that waited outside the door of the reception hall, yanking open the door and bundling Sophie and her yards of white wedding gown inside before ducking in himself.

"Move over, quick!" Marco was laughing like a hyena as he pulled the door of the big vehicle shut and her brother Stefano gunned the engine, carrying them away from the rowdy crowd of their families and friends. Sophie looked back through the window. Her sister Vee, attired in the dusty pink she'd chosen for her maid of honor's gown, waved wildly, blowing her a final kiss and giving her a big thumbs-up.

As she turned around again, Marco leaned forward and

brushed his hands through his thick dark hair, scattering birdseed across the floor of the limo.

She attempted to slide farther across the seat to give him more room, but her dress was caught beneath him. And probably in the door as well. She winced. Oh well, hang the cost. It wasn't as if she were ever going to need it again.

"What are you thinking?" Marco encircled her with his arms, pushing the clouds of her veil away from her face so that he could see her eyes.

She smiled at him, happier than she'd ever believed she could be. "I'm trying to imprint every moment of this day in my mind. I don't ever want to forget one little detail."

"Speaking of forgetting..." Marco's dimpled smile faded, and his black eyebrows drew together in what she could only describe as concern. "Baby, I don't want to pry, but—" he took a deep breath "—have you had a period since you went away? Because I know you haven't had one since you came back and—"

"Oh, my God!" She clapped a hand to her mouth. "I never even thought about it. What kind of an idiot am I?"

"One who had a lot of other serious things on her mind," he said. Tenderly he tipped up her chin, and his dark eyes captured hers, hope and a dawning wonder flaring within them. "I take it that's a no?"

"That's definitely a no," she said. She fell silent, mentally counting. "But we were so careful—"

"Except for that first night," he reminded her. "And the time we spilled the photos—"

"That was months ago!"

He grinned, white teeth flashing in a ridiculously satisfied male smile. "Believe me, I know. One of the things I'm most looking forward to tonight is burning that box of condoms."

She giggled. "If we're right, we won't be needing them for a while."

"Not until next spring, anyway," he said.

They were silent again, a dawning anticipation blossoming between them.

"I have been feeling a little queasy," she confessed. "I thought it was just stress from the wedding."

Marco tightened his arms around her, placing his forehead against hers. "Do you know how happy you make me?" he asked rhetorically.

She smiled gently. He'd enjoyed teaching the summer course and was actually looking forward to the start of the fall semester. And she'd encouraged him to consider some assignments in his field that would take them to different places. Even if he couldn't be exploring new landforms, he could satisfy his wanderlust in some other way.

But they weren't rushing into any decisions. They planned to spend their honeymoon in Hawaii, visiting Jared and Merry during the trip. Then they'd be coming back here to her apartment. He'd already moved in his things—the ones that he hadn't managed to sneak in before she'd gone to Wisconsin—and her sisters had volunteered to clean and bring in all the wedding gifts so that when they came home, they could open them.

But if they were going to have a baby, they'd need someplace bigger—a baby. The reality of it struck her in a sudden rush. "Oh, Marco," she whispered. "A child of our own...."

"I know." He drew back far enough to scan her wide eyes. "Every morning when I wake up with you in my arms, I realize how lucky I am. Most guys never get a second chance. Then again, most guys aren't smart enough to love you." He touched his mouth lightly to hers in a tender pledge that made her heart skip a beat as it did so

often when she thought about Marco. "A baby will
be...incredible," he said. "Something that we've created
together. Our son."

She snorted. "Our daughter, you mean." Then she gave
him a thoughtful look. "Remember that discussion we had
about twins?"

He froze. For a moment his face reflected total, absolute
shock. "I think one at a time will be plenty to deal with.
But—" He shrugged, his eyes twinkling. "I guess we'll
manage whatever we get." His mouth descended on hers,
seeking and finding the sweetness she always gave to him.

"Hey, back there!" Stefano's voice floated back from
the front seat. "Seems to me I had to break up something
like this once before."

She laughed and Marco chuckled. He leaned forward and
lightly cuffed their chauffeur across the back of the head
before reaching for the glass partition and drawing it shut
with a solid thunking sound.

"He'd better get used to it," he said as he pulled his
bride into his arms and resumed where he'd left off when
they'd been interrupted.

*   *   *   *   *

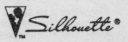

If you enjoyed what you just read,
then we've got an offer you can't resist!

Take 2 bestselling love stories FREE!
Plus get a FREE surprise gift!

SILHOUETTE®

Desire®

A hidden passion, a hidden child, a hidden fortune.

Revel in the unfolding of these powerful, passionate...

SECRETS!

A brand-new miniseries from Silhouette Desire® author

Barbara McCauley

July 1999
BLACKHAWK'S SWEET REVENGE (SD #1230)
Lucas Blackhawk wanted revenge! And by marrying
Julianna Hadley, he would finally have it. Was exacting
revenge worth losing this new but true love?

August 1999
SECRET BABY SANTOS (SD #1236)
She had never meant to withhold the truth from Nick Santos,
but when Maggie Smith found herself alone and pregnant, she
had been unable to face the father of her child. Now Nick was
back—and determined to discover what secrets Maggie was
keeping....

September 1999
KILLIAN'S PASSION (SD #1242)
Killian Shawnessey had been on his own since childhood.
So when Cara Sinclair showed up in his life claiming he had
a family—and had inherited millions—Killian vowed to keep
his loner status. Would Cara be able to convince Killian that
his empty future could be filled by a shared love?

Secrets! available at your favorite retail outlet store.

SDSRT

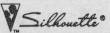